Seven Swords

ARMINDA EISENHARDT

PAGE PUBLISHING
Conneaut Lake, PA

First originally published by Page Publishing 2024

ISBN 979-8-89157-003-0 (pbk)
ISBN 979-8-89157-021-4 (digital)

Printed in the United States of America

I was once told that imagination
is useless. It is knowledge that is way
more important. Although, both go hand in hand.
Whoever reads this book, I want you to know anything
is possible with hope, knowledge, imagination,
and the will to keep going. Even when you feel like you
can't, please enjoy my work and remember you can
do anything you put your mind to, even when others are telling
you, you can't.

SEVEN SWORDS

The ashes burned my eyes. The heat from the flames burned my face. As my mother helped me out of the house, I remembered my father and sister's cold lifeless bodies on the kitchen floor; the arrow that had pierced their hearts would be in my nightmares forever. As my mother held me close to her chest, I could feel her arms embracing me tightly, almost so tight I could barely breathe. I was soon to forget about that as I heard her heart pounding inside her chest. I could hear her breathing heavily as her tears engulfed my face.

I could still feel the burning of the ash in my eyes. The fire soon became a twister of death that covered our house. As she continued to run, I found myself mirrored in the eyes of my mother. I saw eyes that would soon find a life as a worrier. Was this my destiny, a lonely warrior only wanting revenge and death? I looked away from my mother's eyes and away from my reflection, away from the lonely life I saw I would lead.

I had seen enough of my terrified young face filled with tears, sad with grief. I felt my mother stopped quickly as we heard horses roaring back up the road. My mother quickly placed me in the bushes, maybe a mile away from the death-stained ground where our house once stood. Now what stood in its place was a firestorm that started to spread through the forest. The smoke was thick and harsh on my lungs; every time I tried to speak, I found myself coughing hard. It didn't help that I also was crying and could hardly stand the sadness in my heart. I didn't take my eyes off my mother, even though the burning from the ashes wouldn't let me keep my eyes open for too long.

I closed my eyes briefly to try and stop the pain, but I didn't need to open them again. I knew what was to come next; my mother was going to leave me. The thought of losing her pierced my heart like a knife. My mother gently grasped my hand. My eyes swung open, and in an instant, my eyes met hers. I could see the fear in her eyes. As I looked deeper into her eyes, I could see myself and how scared I was. I grasped onto her dress and pulled her closer to me. She inadequately pushed my small breakable hands off her dress as she stood up and spoke.

"I must go. There has been too much death today, my child. You must live, my sweet boy. Please remember I love you, Tadao, and please don't forget me," she said as the tears poured out of her eyes like waterfalls.

My mother walked into the middle of the open space in front of me. I observed in dismay as the men on the horses grabbed her by her hair and hauled her around before getting off their horses only a few feet in front of me. As they started to tear off her clothing violently and rape her, I could feel my fists bleeding from how hard I was squeezing them together. I could feel my fingernails dig into my flesh.

I couldn't hold myself back any longer. I stood up. As I did, a man riding a horse stopped right in front of me. As I looked into his eyes, I could see his eyes burning. His eyes were a crimson color, and the smell of blood was harshly coming off him. I stood frozen as he looked at me coldly. I could still hear my mother screaming as they deflowered her over and over.

"Boy," the man started to say, then paused for a moment. His tone was cold and intimidating to me. I was only ten years old. "Stay down and be silent," he finished.

I didn't want to; it took everything in me to just stand and watch the men hurt my mother. I watched through the bushes from behind the man's horse. Then suddenly he galloped over to the other man and pleaded with them to stop what they were doing to my mother. I looked into my mother's eyes one last time as she lay sprawled out on the ground.

My mother's almost lifeless eyes stared at me, with the gleam of light flashing through them as she mouthed the words "I love you," then the light was completely gone from her eyes, and I knew she was gone. Her lifeless body didn't move, and I sat there, praying that I could see her smile once more. But that was never to be.

The men mounted their horses, but for the one who had never gotten off his horse. Then they took off, back down the road, before sunrise. I ran to my mother's body and held her close to me. I wept as the sun started to raise. Her body was cold and colorless. I was weak and couldn't do anything to save her. My fragile hands were covered in blood and dirt. I hated these seven men who killed my mother. I felt the anger well up inside my heart. It was a burning desire to destroy these men. It burned like the fire that demolished my home in a quick gulp.

Like that fire, I could now feel a blazing storm that filled my heart. I must have sat there for a couple of hours when I finally stopped crying; my eyes were swollen from crying. I noticed the ash started to fall like snow around me. I placed my mother's body lightly back on the ground and walked back to my house. I could still feel the warmth from the wood that was burning sluggishly in the dim light. I found a shovel lying by a tree, close to where the man with crimson eyes was on his horse; he must have left it there for me to find without the other men seeing him do so.

I grabbed my father's body first and dragged it to where my mother's body lay. Then I returned to get my sister's burned corpse as well. I placed her next to our father's. I spent the rest of the day into the next morning burying my family's bodies together so that they would never really be alone. I gathered stones and placed them on top of the fresh dirt I had piled on top of them. After the rocks were carefully placed on the grave, I collected wildflowers, hoping the grave would look beautiful, just like their lives and love were to me.

I looked at my hands, cut and blistered from digging and cutting myself with my nails. But they didn't hurt, not as bad as my heart did. I started to replay what had happened over in my head. I tried to make sense of it all. The more I thought about it, the weaker I felt inside, but also the madder I got. I had to find a way to become stronger and take revenge for what those men had done to my family. I was completely alone, knowing I had nowhere to go, no one to go to. My heart sunk in my chest. I felt my hunger kick in as the sun started to rise. I decided to start walking. I remembered a town my mother used to take me to.

I thought, if only I could make it there, just maybe, I could find someone to help me get food and clothes. The cloth that covered my feet weren't meant for long walks. My shoes had burned up in the fire. I had no choice. My clothing was stained black from the fire. I sluggishly got up off the ground and started to walk. The rocks and branches that covered the ground hurt my feet, but it didn't matter. Nothing did. Right now I was alone. I lost everything that meant anything to me. There was nothing left to lose.

CHAPTER 1

The Stranger (Foe or Friend?)

It was almost nightfall; I didn't notice that I had walked all day. The strange thing was I didn't feel tired. Even the hunger had faded. I didn't feel anything at all but the pain in my soul that lingered on. It was like there was no escape for me. I knew I shouldn't give up, but there was nothing to live for. I stopped my train of thought right away. There was a reason to live. I felt the burning in my heart well up again, to get stronger and avenge my family. I kept walking and thinking to myself, *How am I going to become strong?*

I kept thinking about what I could do to become someone who could save people, not hurt them. Before I knew it, the sun was rising again. I didn't even realize how long I was lost in thought. When I looked up from the ground, I saw a lake in the distance and felt the thirst I had been ignoring arise.

I had never felt a thirst like this before. My throat started to burn from how dry it was. I felt the pain on my lips as I noticed they were dry and broken. I could taste the blood on my lips as I licked them gently to make them feel better but to no avail. It was too late; they were too dry. *I must make it to that lake*, I thought to myself. But then exhaustion poured over me. I must get some sleep first. I found a nice, shady spot in the forest and lay under a tree. Before I knew it, sleep had taken me away from reality, but only for a moment.

I was dreaming about the time when me and my family were happy—my father laughing while I helped him fish for dinner, my mother and sister enjoying watching us make fools of ourselves. Suddenly, just like a flash of light, there was fire all around us. At the kitchen table, I looked over to my sister and my father as the windows broke and watched as their hearts were pierced by arrows. I could feel my heart racing. My stomach started to roll into a ball. I looked for my mother, but as soon as I caught sight of her, she was being pulled out of the house by her hair, and I was all alone in a burning house. I crouched down and covered my head with my arms and screamed at the top of my lungs.

Next thing I knew, my eyes flew open, and cold sweat covered my body. I felt a cool breeze from the night cover me. It felt good, to be honest. I stood up slowly, and I could feel my knees almost give out from under me. I grabbed the tree I was standing next to and tried to focus. My vision was blurred; it must have been because I hadn't eaten anything in what I could think was three, maybe four days. When I looked up, I saw the lake. If I could only make it to the lake, I could catch some fish and get some water. I didn't know how long I was asleep. It felt like seconds, but shortly after I thought about it, the sun started to rise. That morning, the sunrise was like a bright, burning fire to my eyes. I had to cover the rays with my hand. When my eyes finally adjusted to the light of day, I found that the lake wasn't too far away from where I was. So I started to walk, but I strayed from the road and started to walk in the forest instead. I had never been so far from home on my own. The only thing I could think of was revenge and how much I needed something to eat and drink.

I started to remember some of the techniques my father had shown me on how to catch fish so I could start rounding up the supplies when I got there. Suddenly my eyes started to water, and I couldn't hold my tears back any longer. I fell to my knees and cried my eyes out again, just thinking of my family and how they were killed. Why me? Why did they have to die and leave me as the only one left alive? It didn't make any sense.

Even that man made sure I lived. My mother saved me, and I was grateful for her sacrifice, but I yearned to be with them so much. I wanted to follow them. I started to get light-headed and dizzy. The next thing I saw was complete darkness. Maybe I got my wish, and I would see my family. Was I so lucky to be with them again?

When I woke up, I was lying by the lake next to a fire. The heat felt good on my skin. As I looked around, I saw someone in the water. It looked as though they might have been fishing. My vision wasn't back up to par as of yet. When I looked closer, it looked as though they were catching the fish by hand. I looked back toward the fire and noticed a pot boiling. The smell coming from it made my stomach growl loudly. I sat up and noticed a cup of water next to me. I picked it up so fast I think I spilled most of it on myself.

The cold water felt good on my throbbing throat. When I looked up, there was a man standing in front of me, holding a bucket full of fish. I looked closely at the man. He had long black hair tied with a string at the edge of his hair. It looked as though he only tied that little bit to keep his hair out of the way. His hair seemed as though it could go down to his thigh. He had soft crimson eyes that seemed to glow. He was wearing a purple kimono that you could see his muscles through. He was well-built. He looked as though he might have been a soldier.

He had a scar on his neck that started at his Adam's apple and stretched up to his left ear. I sat in silence as I watched him grabbed a bowl and filled it with rice and stew and handed it to me. I could feel the drool starting to flow down my face as I stared at the bowl of delicious morsels. I found myself shoveling the food into my mouth as fast as possible. When I looked up, the man was glancing at me with a huge smile across his face. Then he started to speak in a velvet-sweet voice, manly but kind.

"I'm glad to see you are finally up. You've slept for a week, my friend. Shall I fill your bowl again?" He smiled at me as he took the bowl from me.

"I slept that long? I'm sorry for being a burden on you, sir. Thank you so much for your help," I said as I retrieved the bowl from him.

"How old are you, dear boy?" he questioned me.

"I'm ten, sir," I said.

"You were not a burden at all. I'm glad I found you when I did. You had a fever and didn't look like you would have lasted much longer. So I took you in. Besides, what is a little boy doing out here on his own anyway?" he asked while cleaning the fish he caught when I woke up.

"My…family…was murdered, sir. I thought… I just thought if I could make it to town, I'd be okay," I said as my eyes swelled up with water.

The man's eyes were fixated on me; instead of his eyes being friendly, they were now cold and dim. For a moment, he didn't say anything to me. Then he smiled softly and continued to clean the fish.

"I see. Well, I'll take care of you for now. It isn't safe out here for you to be on your own. Finish eating, then you may rest in the cabin when you are done. In the morning, we will bathe you," he spoke.

"Yes, sir. Thank you again," I said as I scarfed down the rest of the food in the bowl, attempting not to choke.

How ironic is my life right now? I thought to myself. *I almost died again, and yet fate has a way of saving me repeatedly. I'm starting to think there is a reason that I'm still alive… There is a reason I must live, and I have no idea why. Why me?* I thought once again, *Why?*

After I finished my third bowl off, I made my way to the riverbank to clean my bowl. The full moon was bright tonight. I looked at its reflection on the lake. It was so beautiful here, and I didn't even notice until now. The wind blew through my hair, and the trees around us seemed to move as one. I looked down at my reflection in front of me. My short blond hair was stained black from the fire. My body was still dirty as well. I could see where the man tried to clean me up some.

My turquoise eyes were red from the ash and crying so much. My kimono was ripped and dirty from my journey, and my bare feet were now cut up but had a thick green substance pasted on them. The man tended to my wounds as much as he could while I was out. I was so grateful to him for helping me I almost forgot about the fire burning inside my body. But I could never really forget; it was impossible to stop the burning I truly felt.

I made my way up to the cabin, and when I got to the door, the man opened the cabin for me and showed me a bed that I could sleep in. Next to it was a new kimono and a pair of sandals I could wear. It seemed kind of strange that he had prepared all this for me. It was almost like he was expecting me or something. He slowly passed by me and sat in the corner of the room, grabbing his sword and wrapping his body around it as if someone were to come and steal it. I lay down on the white sheets spread out on the floor for me. I didn't realize I was still so tired. Sleep took over my body, and in a matter of minutes, I was out cold.

When I woke up that morning, the man had already gone. I suddenly heard a noise from outside the cabin. When I opened the door, I watched in amazement his sword technique. He would swing his sword so fast it didn't even look like he was moving. When I looked closer, there was some strange purple mist coming from his sword.

The handle was a dragon while the dragon's tail flowed all the way down to the sword's point. He swung his sword again in an effortless and moveless swing, when suddenly a tree fell to the ground. I could see the pearls of sweat drop from his chin. It looked like he wasn't using any effort, but he must have been using an incredible amount to keep his swings precise.

He turned and looked at me when he noticed I was watching him. He smiled softly as he placed his sword back into its sheath. He walked over to me and placed his hand on my shoulder firmly.

"My name is Daichi Takeshi if you are interested. I can train you in swordsmanship. This technique is called Juu Hyaku Ryu," he said with a kind smile.

I could feel my heart pounding like a drum in my chest. This was my chance to become stronger for my family. Daichi was looking at me funny. I guess my face showed the excitement I was feeling. I could feel a smile come across my face as I nodded at him.

"Okay then. Your training will start now. I can see how excited you are to learn. You won't stop moving." He laughed.

I looked at him, confused for a moment, as I watched him walk into the cabin. When he came back out, he was carrying a wooden sword. He walked up to me and handed it to me. I was disappointed. I wanted to learn how to use a real sword. He must have seen the disappointment on my face because he started to laugh. I felt my face get red from embarrassment. I didn't think it was funny at all.

"You must start off with this. I also started with a wooden sword at your age." He laughed; he was laughing so hard he started to cry.

"Okay, this is going to be awesome!" I said, choking on my embarrassment.

"Well, first, I want you to bring twenty buckets of water back here. You must go all the way around the lake. When you get to the middle of the lake, fill up the bucket. Then make your way back here to place the buckets back behind the cabin. Will you please stop looking so disappointed? We have to build your strength before you can learn the sword," he said with a somewhat annoyed tone.

I walked behind the cabin and grabbed the first of the buckets and made my way to the far end of the lake. My legs were burning, and my arms were sore by the time I brought the third bucket back. I saw Daichi preparing something to eat on the fire. He watched me closely. As my stomach started to growl loudly, he laughed as he walked up to me.

"When the last bucket is placed behind the cabin, you may eat," he said as he walked back to the rock. He sat down and continued cutting up the fish and placing the whole bag of rice in the pot.

My stomach was roaring at me. I could see him smirking from the corner of my eye.

I started to feel discouraged. I was so hungry, but I had to finish. If I don't become stronger, I could never be able to honor my family. Maybe this was the reason I was meant to live, to meet Daichi and learn his technique. I couldn't give up when I just started. I had to find the strength inside me to keep going even if it took me all night. I had to focus and get this done not just for me but for my family.

Later, when the sun was burning in the middle of the sky, I was almost done. I had six buckets to go. I was almost back to the cabin when I heard a horse coming up the path. I looked at Daichi with panic on my face. I didn't know if they were coming to get me. I was the only one left alive after all. Daichi looked at me and moved his hand; it seemed like he was telling me to calm down. I didn't know why, but I felt safer when I was with him. I sluggishly started walking to the cabin.

Daichi walked to the opening in the trees where the path ended, readying his sword. He was standing there intensely when the horse broke through the trees. Daichi stood more relaxed and replaced the serious and cold look off his face, smiling at the man. The man jumped off the horse and gave Daichi a hug that I watched Daichi return.

"How is she doing? I bet she is still mad at me, huh?" he questioned the man with a sigh.

"It was for her own safety. She will understand one day, Daichi," he said, trying to reassure him he did the right thing.

This man looked fierce he had scars in his hands that looked like a tiger had scratched him. His hair was tied back into a ponytail, and his eyes glowed green; his facial expression was kind. He must have been from a rich family because his kimono was made from expensive materials. His kimono was red and black. It looked like it was heavy, but it flowed so easily. The red part of his kimono looked like fur, and the black was shiny and smooth. He must have been a soldier from one of the seven kingdoms, but why would he be here, talking to Daichi? Unless Daichi was… At that moment, I was cut off my thoughts by Daichi.

"How many buckets do you have left?" he asked.

"I have six more left, Daichi," I replied.

"You're doing a good job. I think you may be done before sunset," he said with a smile.

I nodded and walked behind the cabin to set down the bucket full of water and grabbed an empty one that laid on the ground. As I reached for it, I heard Daichi and the man go into the cabin. I could hear their conversation as clear as day. I knew I shouldn't listen in, but I was curious to find out what they were talking about and who "she" was. I had to find out what they were talking about. I sat underneath the open window of the cabin. The first one to speak was the strange man.

"Who's the boy?" the man questioned.

"I found him sick and wounded a week and two days ago," he replied with a heavy sigh.

"What about your daughter? You know she wouldn't like to know that you are with another child and can't be with her," the strange man replied with a stern voice.

"What would you rather me do, let the boy die? He has been through a lot the last couple of weeks. I wasn't sure if he would even wake or if he was going to give up on life altogether. He had a long, hard fight, and his soul wouldn't let him give up. My daughter would understand," he said in an irritated yet sympathetic voice.

She is Daichi's daughter. He never said anything about her before, I thought to myself. *Then why can't he be with her?* The more I thought the more questions came to mind, the more I wanted to know. I rolled the empty bucket around on the ground, pondering all the questions I now wanted to ask. I couldn't, of course, because I shouldn't have been listening in the first place, but I wanted to know her now. Was she like her father, kind and gentle? Would she take in a poor boy like me and train me to be stronger? Could she love me? I felt my cheeks get warm, embarrassed of my last thought. I placed my hands on my burning cheeks and shook the thought away. What was I thinking? I shouldn't think of love or a family. I just lost mine. My eyes started to mist over just with the thought of how they died. The stranger started to talk again and made me snap out of my thoughts completely.

"Daichi, I know she would understand, but she misses you. She talks about you all the time, wondering why you haven't come around and why she can't come back to you." He let out a heavy sigh. "I know why she can't, but still, you can't keep her away forever. She will become one of the seven, just like you. There is no fighting it. She will become just like the rest of us whether you like it or not, Daichi. Your sword must be passed down to someone else…" he said loudly.

"No! She will not receive my sword of death. The dragon will be put away as long as I live!" he roared.

"Daichi, you are being unrealistic. The twelve will be taken by someone else whether you like it or not, and your daughter will obtain one of the seven strongest. You are a fool, Daichi, and you know this will happen. Even if you don't like it, she lives in my home.

I will train her to fight. She will be one of the seven. There is no fighting it," he said with no remorse in his voice.

I heard rustling in the cabin and quickly grabbed two of the buckets and ran halfway around the lake as quickly as my little legs would allow me to go. Out of breath, I looked back to the cabin, and as I thought, the stranger was leaving. Him and Daichi had more words. I wish I could hear what they were saying. The look on Daichi's face changed. He looked scared, like something had started that he couldn't stop. He stood his ground as the stranger hopped on his horse and raced off into the distance.

When I got to the other side of the lake to fill the two buckets, my heart felt heavy. Daichi was hiding so much pain and sadness from the world. He couldn't be with his daughter because of something called the seven. His daughter will be forced to be one of the seven. Just the thought of it sent a shiver down my spine. It was something I should fear, but I didn't know why. Like a distant memory that was close but far away, maybe locked away in my heart somewhere, something I didn't want to remember.

I finished before sunset. When I brought the last two buckets and placed them behind the cabin, I sluggishly walked to the front of the cabin and looked at Daichi as he sat on a log, finishing dinner for the night. He looked at me with flames in his eyes, or it might just be the flames from the fire he sat next to. He looked mad and calm at the same time. I forced my aching body to the log beside Daichi and sluggishly sat down beside him. My body was aching all over from the work I did. I felt like I could fall asleep without eating dinner, but I also wanted to take a dip in the lake. I was sure I didn't smell very good.

After dinner, I decided to take a swim. Daichi was already in bed. My whole body was sore, which made the freezing water feels good on my skin. The moonlight made the water sparkle. It was the first time I felt at peace since the men killed my family. When I got out, I saw Daichi holding the sword he said he would never touch again, and from that moment on, we trained.

9

CHAPTER 2

Birth of the Dragon

Eight years had passed since my training had started. Now I had mastered my master's technique, the Juu Hyaku Ryuu. Daichi had a plan for this morning. While I waited for him to wake, I thought taking a dip in the lake would be a clever idea. I was now eighteen. My muscles had grown in quite nicely in my arms and lower body, such as my legs. I still felt like I could have more muscle like Daichi. He would always get all the ladies when we went into town. No one ever looked my way. He was a well-built man. His chest was big, he had a six pack, and his arms looked like he could easily pick up a boulder and throw it.

I knew I sounded jealous of him, and I was. I wish I could have his body anyway. I considered the water. My blond hair was down to my hips. My ocean-blue eyes had grown fiercer with the training, and I knew one day I would have to use it to hurt or even kill someone. I looked over my body as I took my kimono off. I was skinny everywhere. I swore I looked like a woman instead of a man. My body was not where I wanted it, but my body was still strong. I was a lot stronger than I looked. No women would want me like this.

I heavily sighed as I took a step into the icy water. I had been swimming for an hour. It was odd that Daichi hadn't come out yet. It was only daybreak when I woke up. I swam to where my cloth laid on the ground and sluggishly got out of the water and placed my clothes upon my girly figured body. I walked to the cabin and saw Daichi standing in front of the cabin door, looking as though he had seen a ghost. His crimson eyes fixated on the sword he was holding.

"Isn't that…" I said but was interrupted.

"Yes, the dragon sword… I swore…I would never use this sword again. Now is the time to pass it on," he said. The look of sadness and loneliness shot across his face.

"Daichi? What do you mean pass it on?" I asked.

"Someone new must claim his power. I have considered many people… You are the one who should take the dragon and use his power as your own," he said with a frosty tone.

I was confused but at the same time excited. To get the dragon sword would be so cool. Then I was sure the ladies would be all over me, having that powerful sword by my side. Something wasn't sitting in my heart well. If all he wanted to do was give it to me, why was he so sad?

"Are you ready to take the responsibility that this sword holds for you?" he asked.

"Yes, I'm ready, Daichi…" I hesitated.

Daichi turned toward me and pointed the sword toward me. I was shocked. I looked up to Daichi, and his eyes were on fire; you could see the smoke come from his eyes as the flames roared through his eyes. I had no idea what I just got myself into. I closely examined the sword. The handle of the sword was shaped like a dragon. The dragon's tail ran down the sword. It almost touched the tip of the blade. The sword wasn't normal. I could see purple smoke rising from the blade.

"Well, draw your sword, boy!" he yelled in a deep and some-what intimidating voice.

"That voice…" I said, surprised.

It was him that night on the horse, the one who saved me and watched as my mother died horribly. How did I not realize it earlier? He saved me but let her die as those men did what they wanted with her. He just let it happen; he never helped her, not once. Didn't even try to save her, just me. I could feel the hate start flowing throughout my body like a fire I couldn't control. Before I knew it, my body was moving on its own, dueling Daichi.

All my swings were serious swings. My body wanted him dead for what he had done, or should I say, what he didn't do. He could have saved her, but he didn't. I jumped back and started a final attack on Daichi. I lashed at him, and at the last second, Daichi dropped his sword and let me pierce him. I could feel the blood from Daichi's body pour out of him and onto my arm. I let go of my sword in shock. Daichi fell to the ground in what felt was slow motion. It took me a minute to come back to my senses. I just killed my master…

"Boy, your name for now on will be Junjie Manchu. You have earned the power of the dragon's sword. Now, listen to me closely before I die," he said as he coughed out some blood on the ground and dragged himself up to a tree to lean on.

"The responsibility you just took was to take on the seven swordsmen who killed your family. You have taken one out—me, the dragon. The dragon sword, when you pick it up, will change into a weapon just for you. It changes to what your heart chooses. If you are filled with hate, it will be a weapon of mass destruction. It will also change your soul if you choose the path of revenge like I did. When you pick up that sword, you will see everyone with the sign of the zodiac that they are on their forehead. You will only see the ones who have already unlocked their power, by that I mean their weapon. If they have not unlocked their power, then you won't know who they are. From what I heard, they have all been unlocked but for the monkey. So be careful who you trust." He smiled and closed his eyes to never open them again.

I stood for only a moment after he died. I didn't know what to think. I just killed my master. Also, what he said about the sword kept replaying in my mind. I had to be careful when I pick up the sword, but first things first. I pulled the sword out of my master's chest and dragged his body to the lake to clean him up for burial. When I was done cleaning his body, I dragged him to the grass by the cabin, grabbed a needle and thread out of the cabin and stitched the cut that was in his chest, and placed new robes upon his lifeless body.

The same robes I saw him wear the night he saved my life. The regret I felt for killing the man that has always helped me was more than my heart could handle. The rage that took me over in the matter of just minutes was what made me want to destroy him. He was the only one who could save me. This was my destiny. I looked at the sword that was laid on the ground and felt as though I was not ready for the responsibility it had in store for me.

To choose to take on the six that ruined my life from a youthful age, or to turn from this path and maybe fall in love and have a family. As I started to dig a hole to place Daichi's body in, I kept thinking what path I should take. The one I saw was in my mother's eyes before she died or a new path—which one should I choose?

As I placed Daichi's body into the hole, I watched as I started to pour the dirt over his body. His pale face still looked perfect, but there was something different with his face. He always seemed to be in pain or thinking of something. Now he looked completely in peace. What if the other six wanted the same thing, to be at peace for all the wrong that they had done? I thought about the peace I would be bringing to them all.

When I was finished burying Daichi, I grabbed my dagger and cut my hair to shoulder length then pulled it into a bun. I changed my kimono into the special kimono that Daichi had laid on the bed for me. The color was a deep black. It was made of a heavy material but was very comfortable. I slid on my sandals before I walked out the door. Then I looked back at the place that I lived for the last few years. I sluggishly walked out of the cabin and stared at the sword that was still laid on the ground and thought carefully.

If I chose the wrong path, I would be possessed by the sword's anger and become someone I didn't want to be. But at the same time, I knew I wanted revenge for my family. There were two sides of me, one that wanted to be happy and not have to worry about things. As I contemplated on what was more important and which path I must choose for myself, I walked toward the sword and picked it up.

At first, there was nothing. I didn't feel different. I felt normal, then a thought of my mother entered my head, how she was embracing me that night and how the tears rolled down her cheeks. I remembered how much I loved her for saving me that night. When I looked at my right hand that was wielding the sword, it began to change. The dragon moved to the back of the blade and laid its tail on it, the handle of the sword. The dragon itself wrapped its body around my hand. Its golden body was beautiful against the blade of my sword. The head of the dragon faced me, as if he was asking me a question or to see which path I might take. I felt a pain in my right eye, almost unbearable. I dropped the sword on the ground and walk to the edge of the water. I gazed into the water, and my right eye was glowing green, with smoke coming from it. It looked like I had a dragon's eye where my right eye used to be. Shortly the smoke lifted, and my eye was normal again.

I thought nothing of it at that moment. I got up sluggishly and placed the sword in its sheath. I felt different; it was hard to explain, like my whole life finally fell into place. Life had begun for me for the first time. Like everything that once mattered no longer mattered. Only the new path I had chosen mattered. I had no home here anymore. It was time to move on.

I found myself wandering through the forest before long. My sight and senses were more intense. I could see farther than I ever could before and feel the earth tremble under my feet every step I took. I could feel the life of the planet flow through me. I felt stronger than I ever had before. The sword felt heavy on my side, which was the only thing I could feel. For the first time, I felt truly free to do what I wanted. I felt that I was missing something deep down inside, as if everything that was important was pushed aside for a bigger adventure for me. I started to think of my family and how happy we were before that fateful day. How my father and mother would play with my sister, and I remembered my father's name, Junjie Manchu. Live the life of my proud father, and one day I would exceed at what no one else could accomplish.

I was interrupted from my thoughts when I heard a horse coming up the path. I slipped behind a tree, thinking it was the man that came years ago. I peeked out enough to see the road. It wasn't a man at all. It was a woman. Her beauty made me breathless, as her long black hair flowed through the wind. Her face was like a painting that could never be erased out of my heart. Her lips were full and lush. Her eyes were deep brown. She looked as though she was a little older than me, maybe in her twenties, but looked as though she could pass as a teenager. She wore a kimono that was a teal-green color that looked like it was made of silk. As she rode by, it felt like minutes. I looked at her, but it was only a matter of seconds. I knew I had to keep going because of the deed I had just done. I quickened my pace since I knew that at any moment she would probably be looking for the person who killed Master.

I started to run as fast as I could to get to the next town to buy some food and supplies with the money I found by my outfit that Master had laid out for me. I should have been paying more attention to where I was going because suddenly I ran into something. It was hard as a rock and knocked me back. I fell to the ground hard. I looked up and saw a man standing there, looking down at me with a huge smile on his face.

"Well, hello there," the strange man said.

I stared at him in confusion as he gave me his hand to help me up. When I got to my feet, he was still smiling. His orange hair reminded me of a cat; it was messy but was a good look for him. His eyes were gold and looked like cat eyes. He stood about five feet tall, pale skin, looked fragile. He was so thin and brittle. He looked as though he couldn't lift anything, but this man knocked me down. So I knew he was stronger than he looked.

"Hello, sir. I'm sorry I ran in to you." I bowed as I apologized.

"Oh, you're fine. I didn't feel it at all," he said as he laughed.

He then put his hand toward me and smiled his big smile that kind of reminded me of the Cheshire cat in the story Master would tell me when I was a child.

His eyes sparkled as he said, "My name is Light. I have been waiting for you for quite some time, Master."

His orange-gold hair moved through the wind and the light of the sun shined through his golden cat eyes. I reached out for his hand, and he shook my hand so hard and tight I thought my hand would break or be torn off.

"My name is Junjie Manchu. Why have you been waiting for me?" I questioned while I rubbed my arm to make sure it was still there.

"You are the leader of the zodiac warriors. The dragon leads us, am I wrong? I mean you'll have a lot of work to do and fighting to get them to join you." He laughed. "The dragon is the leader."

"The leader of the zodiac warriors?" I stood there, dumbfounded. I thought about the revenge they deserved after destroying my life.

"Yeah, you know very little for taking all this responsibility on," he said with a sigh.

"So which zodiac are you then? Since you know so much?" I questioned.

"I'm the cat...I..." He started to say something but was interrupted by my laughter. "Is there a problem?" I could feel his eyes pierce my skin.

"Um...the cat isn't part of the zodiac anymore...or so I thought?" I said as seriously as possible.

"The cat isn't, thanks to that damn rat. I will get my place back in the zodiac," he said with a grin.

"Light, was it? How can I be your leader if you're not part of it?" I questioned.

That was the wrong question to ask. He picked my six-foot-four-inch body off the ground and over his head with one arm. I was shocked with how strong he was.

"You will help me become part of the zodiac again. If you know what's good for you, Junjie. I am going to get that rat back for what he did to me," he said with revenge on his tongue. I could also see the pain in his eyes.

"I will help you, Light, but please call me Manchu. It's more respectable," I said.

As he sat me down slowly, he smiled again.

"I think I will call you Junjie instead. You call me by my first name. We will be the best of friends anyway. No point in going formal, Junjie." He laughed.

Somehow, I felt like Light was toying with me like a rat in a cage. He was definitely an interesting character. He was also serious about becoming part of the zodiac again. I didn't want to not help him with something he wanted to work toward. Plus, we could work together to gain what we both wanted.

"You think a lot, huh, Junjie?" he said.

"Sometimes, yes. I have a lot to do now that I have this sword by my side," I replied as I grasped the grip of the sword.

"Well, let's get to town. We aren't so far from town now. That's where you were going, right?" Light questioned.

"Yes, I was actually. Let's head out then," I replied.

CHAPTER 3

The Strange Woman and the Interesting Cat

When Light and I had entered town, the sun was setting. Light seemed extremely happy. He always looked happy no matter what unless you mentioned he wasn't part of the zodiac. It was very interesting to me. A part of me wanted to be like him, carefree and lively, but people like that always seemed to have the darkest of pasts. They just held on and kept it all to themselves as the darkness devoured their light inside.

"I found it!" Light said with enthusiasm.

I looked up and saw an Izakaya. Why was Light looking for an Izakaya?

"Why are we looking for a pub?" I questioned him.

"We will need information on the way to the zodiac, right? This would be the best place to get information. Maybe get a couple drinks as well," he replied.

"I guess you're right. We can try to figure out where the first of the seven swords are," I replied as Light turned to look at me and sighed heavily.

"You will have to find all thirteen… You do realize that, right? Why would you only think there were seven?" he asked as he placed a black-and-white bandanna on his forehead and tied back his hair.

"Umm… I'd rather not talk about it," I replied.

Light casually walked in to the Izakaya. I hesitantly followed behind him. When I entered the pub, it seemed normal, several tables full of people from the village having conversations about work and lovers. As I looked through the pub, I saw the bar and decided to go have a drink. Light fit in well. He was already talking to a table full of men, asking about any single ladies he could meet. I took a seat at the bar and looked up at the bartender.

"What would you like to drink?" he asked in a husky voice.

He looked as though he hadn't had a bath in weeks, maybe a month. His white clothes had black stains all over them, some big, some small. He had pimples all over his face, oily skin, and dirty black hair.

"Some water please," I replied.

"You only want water?" he asked.

"Yes, please," I replied.

"He would really like some baijiu," said a beautiful voice from behind me.

She came close to me and put her face right next to my ear and whispered with a silky voice, "That will give you more of a kick than water will."

I turned quickly to look at her, and our lips touched. My heart was pounding. I could feel it trying to escape my chest when I saw who it was standing in front of me. That woman from earlier. I could feel my emotions taking over my body as I reached out for her and kissed her luscious lips. I wished she could be mine forever. When I opened my eyes, her face was bright red, and her brown eyes sparkled brighter than before.

"Who do you think you are to touch me like that?" she questioned as she stood up and placed her fingers to her mouth, still blushing.

"I…I'm sorry. I don't know what came over me… You're just so beautiful I couldn't stop myself. I'm very sorry, ma'am," I said, embarrassed by what I just did.

She looked at me, shocked, as she moved her arms down to wrap them around her breasts, which—I wasn't going to lie—were perfect in every way. She still stood to the side as I examined her curves. Her body was beautiful. I couldn't stop imagining touching her soft skin. Her butt was breathtakingly huge as well. Just looking at her made me want her more and more.

"You think I'm beautiful? Why are you looking at me so intently, sir?" she asked.

"I'm sorry, but your beauty is just breathtaking, ma'am," I replied.

She suddenly walked up to me and kissed my lips gently. Her hands touched my face with grace. I could feel the warmth of her breath on my lips. The deeper and more passionate the kiss got, I could barely breathe.

When she stopped kissing me, she moved her head next to my ear and said, "My name is Sachiko Saki. I will stay by your side as long as I'm wanted." Then she stood up again and placed money on the table for my drink and walked to the back of the pub and sat at an empty table.

I faced the bartender, trying to breathe and collect myself. My heart was still racing.

"You're a lucky man. She has never kissed anyone before. She's the daughter of the famous Daichi Takeshi," he said.

"What! Takeshi?" In a matter of seconds, my heart dropped.

"What's wrong? You look like you saw a ghost?" he questioned.

I grabbed my drink and chugged it down. I regretted doing it right away. I started to cough uncontrollably. I looked to my right, and there was Light with a huge grin on his face. I could feel my face burning.

"W…what?" I questioned him.

"Why's your face so red? You don't even need to answer it. The whole place saw your make-out session." He laughed uncontrollably.

All I could do was turn away and look down at the table. It didn't matter. We could never be together. I killed her father. I didn't get how life was adding up for me. I fell for the daughter of the man I killed. How ironic. She said she would never leave my side, so did that mean she might already know what I did to her father? She was just waiting for the right time to attack. I'd have to keep myself away from her emotionally and physically.

"Earth to Junjie," Light said.

"Huh, oh, I'm sorry. What are you saying?" I replied.

"I heard she is quite famous around these parts. She is a princess, but she would prefer to help this village from the zodiac. The Ox—we found the first one," he said with excitement in his voice.

"She fights the Ox on her own?" I asked, surprised.

"She's quite strong, the villagers say. She keeps her at bay," he said.

"The Ox is a woman?" I asked.

"What, did you think they were all men? When the time comes, the zodiac members have to pass down their weapons to the next person of their choice. If they don't, the zodiac sign automatically transfers to someone it chooses. Oh, and she fights with a halberd, so now we know what we need to know," he said as he smiled.

For the first time, when he smiled, I saw his two little fangs. I never realized how much he really looked like a cat till right now. So I had a cat. Twelve more to go. I could feel myself sigh heavily.

"We can do this, buddy. Don't put it past us," he said as he smiled.

"I was just hoping that they were men, not women," I said as I found my eyes wandering to the corner of the room where she sat alone.

"If you want her so much, go gets her, then you don't have to stay here with me. Besides, I would enjoy another show." He laughed.

I thought about it for a moment, the warmth of her skin against mine. Somehow, it just brought my mind in to the daydreaming mode. Thinking of how our lives could be together, how our family would be, and other things along those lines. I could hear my heart pound in my ears. The one thing I couldn't shake was thinking of holding my newborn baby in my arms. I could only imagine how that might feel. The joy and how scared I might be in the long run, but how precious a gift a baby would be. I quickly snapped back into reality when I heard the door slam against the wall of the pub. I looked over to see who had entered. It was a woman, fair-skinned. My eyes were automatically drawn to her symbol on her forehead, the Chinese symbol of the Ox. Her hair was pulled up into two buns

21

on top of her head. There was a red ribbon tied around both. Her face was young, but she also looked angry. Her body was thin and curvy. She wore a qipao; it was loose and wide. The center was held by a wide belt that was wrapped around with lace. As she walked, she looked like she was floating on air. I was surprised she could be so graceful but mad at the same time. We watched her walk to the back of the pub, to the woman I wanted to make mine forever.

"Who do you think you are, keeping me from attacking this village?" she yelled at Saki.

"I wouldn't have to stop you if you would just stop attacking the villagers," said Saki with her beautiful, soft voice.

I started to notice that the villagers started to leave the pub. The only people left inside was Light, the bartender, Saki, the Ox, and I. I could start to feel the tension rise when the Ox slammed her hand down on the table and busted it in half. There was so much dirt and dust moving around I couldn't see Saki. I felt myself jump up out of my seat as I tried hard to locate her. When it cleared, I was surprised. Saki was gone. The Ox was surprised in her rage. She threw the table in Light and I's direction. We both jumped in opposite directions to avoid the table. I had jumped to the right. I quickly looked to the bartender, who looked untouched by the attack. I stood up; I was done with this violence. I could feel my eyes burn and my hand grip the handle of my sword.

Saki jumped from the beams that held the ceiling of the pub together and did a flip, landing behind the Ox. She grabbed the Ox by her hair and swung her around and through the wall of the pub with ease. Then she looked our way and bowed. We found her running out of the hole she had made in the wall.

Light grabbed me by the arm and rushed us outside. Maybe a little too enthusiastic about the whole thing, he was laughing the whole time. He dragged me out of the building. He was also kind of skipping as well. When we got to the area where Saki and the Ox were fighting, all we saw at first was the Ox flying and landing in some trees in front of us. Saki's beauty was even more animated than I could ever imagine. The sun on her body was soft and smooth, just like the way she felt when she touched me. My new idea of her was strong and rough. She was always fighting the Ox on her own without help. She must have had a hard life. The Ox stood up and looked at Saki.

"Fang, don't you ever get tired of losing against me?" said Saki.

"Saki, I know you have some gruesome scars from me as well on your body." She laughed.

Fang raised her hand, and out of nowhere, a giant axe materialized. The axe was beautiful and made of gold and silver. The detailed ox that covered the blade was very detailed. You could see every muscle and vein on this beast. Fang started to run toward Saki. I was quite fast and wasn't going to let Saki fight alone anymore.

As Light stood there for a moment, he didn't notice that Junjie had left his side. He was so wrapped up in the intensity of the battle. As he watched the Ox make a full attack toward Saki, a dust cloud formed around her.

"Man, did you see that the Ox isn't someone to play with?" he said as he looked to where Junjie should be standing in confusion. "Wait, where did you go, Junjie?" he asked as he looked toward the dissipating dust cloud.

Light

Standing between Fang and Saki was Junjie, holding Fang's attack away from Saki. The look on Saki's face was of surprise. Junjie's eye was burning green, and his other eye was still blue like the ocean. Light stood there with his mouth wide open, trying to grasp the fact Junjie had even moved. Junjie pushed the Ox back with one swing of his sword. As the Ox flew back, she did a backflip and landed on her feet. She was staring intently at Junjie. She was ready to fight to the death, and the look on Junjie's face showed the same thing.

"Listen to me, Fang. Either you can join me or die. It is your choice," said Junjie as he smiled for the first time I had seen so far.

"Join you? I'm confused by what you mean by that. Why would I join a stranger?" She laughed, then focused on the sword Junjie was holding. Her face was pale before, but she looked like a ghost now.

"You can join me and live or die by my hand, whichever you would prefer," he said in an ominous voice. I had never heard Junjie talk like this before.

I paused and looked at Saki. She also noticed the sword and fell to her knees. I noticed the tears filling her eyes. She held her hand to her mouth to silence her cries. She must have noticed something about the sword, or she was just happy that Junjie saved her. I didn't know how to take it.

"You...ar...are the leader of the zodiac warriors," Fang said in a scared voice.

I could see the hazy green smoke coming off Junjie's eye; the mist became stronger. I could see Junjie get irritated with waiting for her to fight or give in to him. He wasn't taking her playing with him lightly. Also, at this point, I had come to realize that Junjie had a much deeper, darker side to him than I had ever seen before. A rage that couldn't be fed. This look in Junjie's face was terrifying. For the first time, I was honestly happy that I was on his side and not the one standing in front of his sword.

"Have you made your choice yet, Ox?" he questioned in a harsh voice.

"I have. I will not join you unless you can beat me, Dragon." She laughed.

"Well then, prepare yourself to fight," he said while positioning himself.

He placed his left foot in front of him and his right foot gently beside Saki so as to protect her from the blow that he was getting ready to use on Fang. I saw Fang's life drop out of her face when she realized that he would fight her no matter what. She was unwilling to accept the fact that he was willing to go to any length to get what he wanted. Even though I wasn't sure what that was, besides getting her on our side. Before I could make another thought, the dirt was roaring like a whirlwind in front of me. I could barely see Junjie; that's how quick he was moving, dodging and attacking Fang. I could see the green mist coming from Junjie's sword with every attack he made. That's pretty much all you could see of Junjie, the neon-green mist and light coming from his sword. I could hear Fang desperately trying to dodge Junjie's attacks, doing backflips and jumping from tree to tree. Even that didn't help her. He was way too quick for her. Before she would make it to where she was going, he was already there to attack her. Finally, the whirlwind subsided, and the air was clear again. Junjie had Fang pinned against a tree, with his blade deathly close to her neck. Her clothing was torn. Her dress now looked like a piece of cloth. The only parts of her body that were covered were her torso and thighs. Her body was covered in cuts. The deepest one was on her forehead. Blood dripped down her face to her right shoulder.

"If I refuse you, Dragon?" she questioned, taking a heavy breath in.

"Guess?" Junjie said as he moved the sword closer to her throat.

She gasped for air because of Junjie's body being so close to hers and the tree. I'm sure he was crushing her fragile body, with all his power pressed up against her.

"F...fine... I...will join you," she said in an airy, raspy voice.

Junjie placed his sword slowly into his sheath and moved the pressure of his body off her slowly. As he did this, she sluggishly fell to the ground.

"Light?" said Junjie.

"Yes, Junjie?" I replied.

"Take her into the pub and get her new clothes please," he said, this time looking at me. His neon eye started to fade.

"Yes, I can do that," I said quickly.

I picked Fang off the ground quickly. I was surprised how light she was. I kind of felt like a pervert holding a pretty much naked girl in my arms. I felt my face get hot. I had to look and make sure Junjie didn't see how embarrassed I was. He luckily was helping Saki off the ground. So I made haste to get Fang into the pub and rushed off to get clothing for her.

Junjie

"Are you okay, Saki?" I asked.

"Yes, I'm fine, Manchu," Saki said with hesitation.

25

I reached my hand out to her and waited for her to reach out for my help up. She hesitantly reached up for my hand. Her hand was so soft and fragile in mine. Our eyes met for a moment. For some reason, she quickly broke our eye connection and with her left arm. She covered her chest as I helped her to her feet. At this point, I knew something was wrong. I didn't know what I did. I was forcing back the feeling of wrapping her in my arms and comforting her. I also knew I should hold back these feelings from her. I knew the life I chose was one that love could never follow. This life was meant to be a lonely one. I was meant to be alone. Next thing I knew, she was holding me in a deep embrace. I moved my arms slowly from my side to wrap around her warm body. I had never felt an embrace so warm and loving from anyone before. I found myself falling into this feeling that was forbidden to me.

CHAPTER 4

This Thing Called Love

The moments we stood like this felt like forever. I fell more in love with her without meaning to.

"Saki?" I said.

"Yes, Manchu," she replied, looking up at me.

"We should stop this before it becomes something more than we are willing to endure," I said with a pause as I swallowed hard, trying to stop my heart from racing. "I mean we could never really be together, not really, not now, not in a world where we must fight to survive like this. Also…" I tried to continue, but she stopped me by placing her finger over my mouth.

She moved her hand to my face as she rubbed her forgiving fingers on my cheeks. I had to hold back what I felt for her. Then she kissed my lips softly. She wasn't holding anything back, not one feeling she had for me. I could feel the love she had for me in her kiss. I had to push her back before the feeling could get any stronger. Her eyes looked through me like I was an open book. Like she knew that I was already feeling the connection we had. It confused me because I never thought I would love someone as much as I loved this woman standing in front of me. Was it something the sword had given me? A passion for the person my master longed to see for a very long time. Was it possible to gain emotions from the master of the sword before? All I knew for now was, this couldn't happen; it could never work out. If she ever found out that I killed her father, I would never see the love in her eyes ever again. I must stay quiet about how I feel and not give her anything to regret later. I looked away from her to only be pulled back into an embrace. I found myself lost in my feelings. I pulled her arms from me and started to walk back toward the pub on my own.

When entering the pub, I saw that Light had gotten the Ox new clothes and was washing the blood from her body. He was doing his best to wrap her injuries and make sure they wouldn't get infected. Light looked up and noticed me.

"Hey, Junjie!" He smiled.

"How is she holding up?" I asked.

"She is holding up well actually. She was probably worn out more from the beating Saki gave her than the damage you caused." He laughed.

"That's good to hear. We should leave her here and move on to the next zodiac on the list," I replied.

"She is with you know. We should at least wait till she wakes. At least to tell her what our plans are." Light disagreed with me.

"Fine, I suppose you are right about that." I sighed heavily and sat down at the bar.

I looked up at the bartender and saw he was looking at the door. There Saki stood, staring at me, or so I thought. She walked right past me and sat at the end of the bar. It looked like her and the bartender had something to talk about. Both looks on their faces were serious. I watched in curiosity as the bartender left and walked toward the end of the bar to speak to her.

As they talked, I decided to make my way to the table Light sat at to see how he was doing. He seemed kind of nervous when I had asked him to take Fang into the pub earlier. I sat next to Light and waited only a moment before he started to talk.

"You noticed, didn't you?" He sighed.

"Noticed what, Light?" I questioned.

"That I was nervous earlier." He gave out a heavy sigh then continued. "That was the first time I have ever held a naked woman in my arms. I wasn't sure how to react. I knew she needed help and needed new clothing, but I am still a man. I hope this doesn't make our friendship any different," he said as his golden eyes shot up at me.

"What? No, that wouldn't change anything." I looked at the table Fang was sprawled across.

"I would have killed her, you know that, right?" I asked hesitantly.

"Yes, I know that…" he said heavyheartedly. "Nonetheless, we need to be that way in times of war. Because if we aren't, we could fall to someone's blade just as easily. So don't worry about that so much. The zodiac just gets stronger from here," he replied with a laugh.

I found myself look back to Light and the smile on his face. I realized in that moment Light wasn't going anywhere; he was with me for the long haul. I felt more at peace and smiled back at Light.

"You know, Junjie, you should smile more. Don't let the tough times get you down," he said as he jumped up. "Fang is awake. At least speak to her."

I looked over, and sure enough, she was sitting up, holding her head where I had cut her. She sluggishly got off the table and sat in a chair next to it. She looked up to me with a cold, frosty look in her eyes. Her eyes were like the color of grass covered in the frost of the winter mornings. Her skin was white as snow, but I could feel the heat come off her.

"So you are the new leader of the seven?" she said.

"Yes, I am. My name is Manchu Junjie…" I replied.

"Pure, handsome…" she said.

"What?" I said, confused for a moment.

"Your name doesn't suit you, Manchu. You may be handsome, but you are no longer pure," she said as she looked over to Light, who was sitting to her left.

"What is that supposed to mean?" I said in a frustrated tone.

"You are telling me you haven't noticed?" she replied coldly.

"Noticed, what are you talking about?" I was starting to get mad.

"Your eye. Don't you feel the heat in your eye when you get ready to fight? When you are ready to kill someone? The rage that fills

29

your body when you're wielding that weapon?" she replied sharply as her look cut through me.

I never thought about it before. That was my first time wielding the sword in a fight. I did remember how it felt when I became the master of the dragon sword though. It was painful, like my body was being devoured by the sword and the rage and feelings of the sword itself. Maybe that was why I felt so strangely. Maybe you could take into yourself what the sword desired. Maybe not only what you desired but what every master desired before you. If that was so, no matter what I thought when I picked it up, my pure side would still have been corrupted no matter what. So who was I? Was I a man who was in love with Saki, or was I Just a man being taken over by a sword?

"You finally realized you are evil to a point… I am astonished that you haven't been as corrupted as all the other leaders though. One of your eyes only changes. Normally, both eyes turn red, but only yours turn green. How intriguing," she said with confusion.

"So what's that mean exactly?" I interrogated.

"You may have more control over yourself than other leaders have," she answered.

"So Junjie may be a special case then?" Light asked with enthusiasm.

"You could say that," she responded. "I'm sure you three plan on doing this alone?"

"Three?" Light asked with confusion.

"Yes, Manchu, the Cat boy, and Saki," she replied. "You are in love with her, right, Manchu?"

I didn't know how to answer, or maybe I just didn't want to. Fang noticed my hesitation and the most likely confused look on my face when she had asked that question. She started to laugh loudly, which caught the attention of Saki. When Fang noticed, she stopped laughing and turned back to being serious.

"You two are fated by the stars. That's why you both have fallen for each other so quickly. I have never seen her look at anyone that way. When a man wants her, she normally just walks away and pretends they don't exist. So take love when you have it, even if you feel like you don't deserve it. It's already yours. You must choose what to do with it in the long run. Lose it or keep it. It's your choice at the end of the day," she said. "Your next closest target is the Tiger. He lives in a large town. A week's walk from here, four days if you take a horse. It's a town called Toma. He is as vicious as an animal. He'll not stop till you are dead. Just forewarning you." She laughed.

Light and I both looked at each other. We couldn't see how this was funny, but we knew we had to keep moving forward. This meant, if we died, we would have to do it fighting. There was no way out once we started. We must finish this. I was only on the second of the zodiac, and I had to fight one of the strongest next, which made me realize he must be one of the seven I must face head-on.

"So I guess we will be heading out then. Thank you, Fang," Light said.

"How will I keep in contact with you once we leave? What if I need your assistance?" I asked quickly.

"Once I have joined you, my weapon will notify me when you need help, Manchu. I don't see that you will need my assistance though," she said as she stood up.

"Why is that?" I asked.

"Because you have Saki," she replied as she took her leave from the pub.

Saki stood up and made her way toward Light and I. She was smiling. I could feel my heart skip a beat. Her smile was soft and sweet and warmed me from inside. When she got to us, she stood next to Light. Light was a little confused as to why she was standing next to him. I could see him getting a little uneasy as he looked at me. Like I would cut him down if he even looked at her, which made me laugh a bit.

"What's so funny, Junjie?" Light said forcefully.

"Nothing. Everything is well. Shall we go then? I think we have everyone," I said as I couldn't help but smile.

"Yes, let's go," said Saki in her sweet yet settled voice.

We made our way out of the pub and through town. We had stopped at the marketplace in town to buy some food and other needed items, such as blankets, a flint and cloth, and other necessities we needed to camp at night and stay warm. The villagers were so pleased with us defeating the Ox they pretty much just gave us everything we wanted. It was nice to see what we had accomplished for one village and how happy the townspeople were to not have to worry anymore.

When we were done at the market, we made our way to the road to start our journey together. For the first time, I felt like everything was going to be okay. I still had the pain in my heart of what would happen if Saki had ever found out I was the one who killed her father. For now, I would push that aside and keep ahold of love till I found a reason not to.

We made our way into the forest to find a camp for the night. When we finally found a place, we were all so hungry we made a fire and made a fish stew. As we all sat around the campfire and ate our meal before bed. We made Light talk of our route in the morning and how we would keep it at a week to get there, trying not to stray off task too much, as Light put it.

I had woken up around midnight that night to find Saki sitting up, staring at the moon. Next thing I knew, I was next to her, looking at her soft skin and beautiful hair glowing in the moonlight. Her eyes sparkled like fireflies when she looked at me.

"You know, Manchu, your eyes are beautiful. They remind me of the ocean when it is calm and untainted," she said as she smiled at me.

"Do they now?" I smiled back.

"Yes, you are always in so much pain, but your eyes do not falter from your pain. They are untouched by the world," she said as she wrapped her arms around her knees and placed her head in between them.

"You really think so?" I replied.

"Yes, Manchu, I do," she said as everything fell silent.

"Um… So what are you doing up so late?" I asked as she raised her head to look at me.

"I couldn't stop thinking," she replied.

"Is there anything I can help you with?" I asked she smiled softly at me.

"Actually, I was wondering what it's like to be with someone…
you know, like sexually…" She blushed. "I mean, like how that feels.
You know, like when it's real," she said shyly.

"Um…I don't know. I guess it will feel amazing, like you were
the only two people on earth and nothing could ever stop you from
being near each other even when you have to be far apart," I answered
as I looked at the moon.

"One day I want something like that, something real and not
meaningless," she said shyly.

"Me too," I replied.

I couldn't look at her because I knew I might not be able to
hold myself back, and not knowing what was to come or even if these
feelings I had were mine, I knew I wouldn't be able to stop myself if I
touched her skin or kissed her soft lips again. I could feel the tension
build between us, but I couldn't take her, not now, even if I wanted
to.

"Do you think sex is meant to be deep and meaningful?" she
asked without hesitation

"I do. It is connecting on a higher level, building up on emotions, and connecting us on a whole different level. It's different than
being physical or even being emotional. I believe people who truly
love each other should be that committed to each other," I said without thinking.

"Us?" she said, surprised.

"I…I mean other people… You know, like people who want to
be together forever… Not like people who just met." I found myself
trying to find ways around it.

"Oh, yeah, I guess you're right," she said sadly.

She sluggishly got up and kissed my forehead and found a spot
far away from where I was sleeping to lay down for the night. I found
myself tossing and turning most of the night as I thought about our
conversation with her that night. My mind was lost in a black hole of
thoughts. I couldn't escape, not even if I wanted too.

The next morning, I awoke to Saki gone. I panicked as I threw
my body forward like I was almost giving myself whiplash. I looked
back and forth, frantically trying to find her. I stood up quickly and

looked for Light; he was gone as well. *What was going on, and why would both be gone?* I thought to myself, a little jealous because she could have been mine if I wasn't so proud. I shook my head hard to erase the images of them together out of my mind. I packed my bag with my bedding and swung it over my shoulder. *I will track them,* I thought to myself, but I didn't have to go too far. A mile into the forest, I had found both of them. They were facing each other, sitting in the middle of a circle. The circle was made up of quartz crystal and branches. They both sat with their legs crossed and hands comfortably placed on their knees. The sun shining through the trees reradiated off the crystals, making Light and Saki glow.

When I reached the spot where they sat motionless, Light opened his eyes and looked toward me. I was still hidden by the trees. I could vaguely see Light, but I saw his eyes sharpen, and he was staring in my deration with a smile on his face. I saw him lean forward into Saki. I saw their lips touch—at least that's what I thought I saw. It made me want to hurry over to them to see what was really going on. I tripped over a branch while trying to get to them and ended up falling into Saki's lap.

I could feel the smooth fabric of her kimono on my face. Today she was wearing one that was much thinner, not so heavy, which made since it wasn't as cold as it was last light. I didn't want to turn around and look at her face. I ended up moving sluggishly around till my back touched the rough ground. When I looked up at her with my head still in her lap, the first thing I saw was a bright light. The next thing I saw… Oh god, I felt so bad. Saki was holding up the front of her kimono. Her boobs were in my face. She was trying to keep her kimono together without it coming completely open. She struggled to hold herself in her kimono. I quickly went to move and ended up making her lose what she was holding. Next thing you know, she was completely undressed, sitting in front of me. I quickly moved my body in front of her so she had some kind of cover.

I looked up to catch Light's eyes. They were beaming like he might have had too much catnip for one day. His nose started to bleed heavily.

"Junjie, you don't have to hide her. I already know what she looks like," he said as he started to laugh wildly.

He must have seen the look I gave him because he was no longer laughing; he was more like a wounded kitten now. I sighed heavily, glimpsing back at Saki to see if she was fully dressed yet. By the time I looked, she had just finished tying her kimono back together.

Saki looked at me with her beautiful eyes and said, "I'm sorry you missed it. I can get my clothing back on pretty quickly. Maybe sometime in private I could show you." She slowly got up and walked to the edge of the lake.

I could feel my face start to burn. She couldn't be serious; I mean, come on, she was way too good for me. She could do so much better than the likes of me. *I mean I am better than the cat boy*, I kept thinking to myself as a smile came across my face.

"You know she's way out of your league, right?" Light said as he leaned up against a tree.

"What do you mean?" I laughed it off like I didn't already know that.

"Junjie, seriously, she is a woman. You should never touch someone you will play like a toy. She has more goals and responsibilities than you have ever had. If you toy with a woman like that, with how unattached you are to your emotions, it could end very bad, Junjie," Light warned.

"I mean, it's not like I could ever love her anyways, so why not have some fun." I laughed, but Light didn't find the humor in it.

"Junjie, you will see in time that you will mess up with something that could be perfect, but when you have the chance to make it right, you will choose to walk the other way out of fear and lose everything." Light smiled. "On a brighter note, I have never seen her naked and would prefer not to, so don't worry about me. I am not after her." He laughed.

"Not funny, Light." I laughed, trying to erase his warning from my mind.

35

CHAPTER 5

The Forsaken Night, the Beginning of the End

"So I guess we should be moving forward in this journey! Saki, it's time to go." Then he looked to me, watching her. "Heed the warning I gave you. She may love you, but you don't care for her the same and never will." He sighed.

"I'll be fine, Light. She will hurt more than I ever will. So I don't have to worry about the pain, only she will. I am not worried about losing her. I just don't like the idea of other men looking at her," I said.

"Junjie, what am I going to do with you?" He sighed and was very pleased with what I said as he rolled his eyes.

What? I don't want him to think there will be anything special she came onto me, so I'll let her have what she wants for a bit till I find the one I am meant to be with. Piece of cake, or so I thought.

We finally got out of the woods and found ourselves in a village. I was super excited but realized Saki and Light were nowhere to be found. So I made my way to the inn. *Maybe they are there*, I thought.

"Saki, trust me. Stay away from Junjie. He is no good for you. He brings you death, not life," said a mysterious voice.

"If he truly loves me, I will sacrifice my life for him," said Saki with passion.

"You are a stupid girl. He will use you and throw you away the second he doesn't want you anymore. He isn't interested in loving you. He is only interested in his selfish ways and his needs. You are at the bottom of his list, Saki, believe me," the voice pleaded with her.

Saki

I stood there for a moment and held my hand to my chest and thought about the way he looked at me and the way he blushed, the way his hands touched my skin that one time. Thought to myself, *He won't be like the others. I know for a fact he loves me, and I would use all the strength I have and even my life to prove it. You know the saying, I wish I knew then what I know now? Well, I wish I never thought with my feelings and my heart and used my mind.* To be continued…

"He wants to be with me. I know that more than you will ever know. Now stop trying to push me away from him, please," she begged.

"Foolish girl, if you are willing to risk all that you are for nothing in return, then be my guest. I will not stop you. One day, you will know the truth, and you will see the man you chose is nothing but a scared, foolish man who will walk away when he is most needed."

My feet were moving before I realized it. My heart didn't want to hear any more. *How could he know what he is like? How could he see what I see? He isn't me, so he can't know.*

All these warnings to stay away, and yet I find myself wanting to know the true him. The man he truly was deep down inside. The one I was starting to care about maybe more than I should, my heart wouldn't let me betray him. This foolish heart I had inside me wanted me to hold him close to me.

* * * * *

Light found himself lost in town, trying to find the inn. He never worried about being lost. He could always find his way around town. He couldn't help but follow a smell that brought a sweet scent to his nose. He followed the path to a long stairway that went up a hill; it looked steep and narrow. It was hidden well by the shadows. As Light looked up this dark path, he saw a woman caped. She looked as though she was flowing above the world. With a cheerful expression, he was way up the path. The closer he got to the end of the path, the colder it got. He could feel the hairs on the back of his neck stand up. When he reached the top, he saw a well. Below the well, on the ground, were growing lilies, which was odd to Light. As he walked closer to the well, he saw a figure of a woman standing beside a tree. He quickly turned and looked away from her. As his back was turned away from her, he sat on the well and crossed his arms. He closed his eyes and began to talk.

"What do you want with us?" he questioned in a serious tone.

"I'm sure you know what we want," she hissed through her teeth.

"Yes, I do, actually," he replied.

"You are here to turn us against our leader, Junjie. You cannot sway the heart so easily, evil one. I have seen how this story ends for him. It is up to him to figure out what he chooses to do with the choices he has at play here. One ending is sad, the other he finds what he has always wanted…" Light sighed heavily.

"You are even unsure what the future holds for that man with the cold heart." She laughed with a hiss.

Light stood up and turned to the figure, now seeing her blood-stained eye. He slammed both of his hands down hard on the well. His eyes glowed like burning amber as he looked at her with the utmost hate, like an enraged cat hunting for his prey, that he had already lost more than once.

"Oh, it looks like I have finally got the cat's attention," she hissed in a cold tone that would make anyone's blood run cold.

"You listen here now, Amanda. You are no better than that hate that is taking Junjie's heart. Because I hope he gets his happy ending doesn't mean he will have it." He turned his head to the left and started to cry. "He… He could make the wrong choices, but who am I to get in the way of a future? He may turn away from it. It isn't my place. I will be beside him either way…" he said as best he could through the tears.

"So you know she dies then?" She laughed.

At this point, Light looked up at her, shocked, with tears running down his face. His eyes turned cold and lifeless only for a moment. *She couldn't know what would happen to Saki. She couldn't know what would come. Junjie's pain, Saki's sacrifice, the horrible details of what was about to come. There was no way they could know what I have seen and hold close to my heart in the midst of all this. The future was mine to hold on to, not theirs, something I have to hold on to and protect with my life.*

"How!" he shouted.

"How do we know this? Light, you of all people should know how we know." She grinned a hellish grin.

Light could say nothing; he only stood there in shock. Thoughts of the past started running through his head. He started to shiver in fear. His vision became blurry and started to fade to black. He felt like he was getting nauseous as the world started to spin around him. He could barely breathe; his heart was racing so fast you could see it pounding in his chest. He found a moment where he could focus enough to look up and saw she was already gone. The sweet smell had turned into the smell of rotting corpses and blood.

* * * * *

Junjie

As I wandered through the town, still wondering how I lost Saki and Light, I had finally found the inn. The doorway was well lit by the two lanterns that hung dangling on both sides of the entrance. The door was made of a fine piece of oak, painted white, with two tigers embracing each other on the door, a cub curled up between them. The building looked like it had gold trimming. The beams that held it up was cut in a spiral matter. It looked as though the inn was about five floors high.

At that moment, all I could think about was Saki and how beautiful she was. How nice it would be to hold her close. I didn't know why I was thinking this way. *How does she feel for me? How can I show her how I feel? Is it too soon to feel this way? Is it weird to think of a future with the path I am on? Is it even possible to have a future ever, the way I am now? I have nothing to offer her, no house, no money. Can she still love me? What am I thinking? I have a job to do, a mission I must complete before I can do anything like that. A future though... Can be a nice thought to hold on to though.*

I found myself walking into the inn. When I opened the door, you could tell it was heavier than it looked; it felt like it could weigh a ton. There were ten round tables on the left side of the inn closest to the bar. The bar wrapped around to the counter to check in. From the door, the counter was about fifteen feet away from me. I walked up to the counter. There was a sign-in book and a golden bell that you could ring if no one was there to help you. I started to look around and looked at the flattop table that was in front of me. It stood to my waist. I was in no hurry but starting to worry about my companions. They had been gone for quite some time.

When I was about to ding the bell, the inn door opened, and in came Light and Saki. It looked as though they were having an intense conversation. I had never seen Light not smiling or making fun of something. When Light saw me looking at them, his intense face became soft and cheerful again. I knew something was wrong. Now more than ever, when they came closer, I saw Light's face seemed pale and somewhat lifeless even though he was smiling. Saki walked up to my left side, and Light on my right. I looked down at Saki, but she only looked down to the left and to the floor, never raising her head to look at me. I looked to Light, who was looking right at me, smiling, but his cat eyes looked more fierce than normal. I kept racking my brain to think of something I could have missed, but nothing I could think of. I mean, they were gone for a while, but what could change them this much?

I was about to speak to Light when the counter clerk came from the bar to help us. She was wearing a short pink kimono that had white lacy trim. Her hair up in a bun. She had a round-looking baby face that was soft on the eyes.

"May I help you?" she asked in a sweet, soft tone.

"Yes, may we please get a room?" I asked as Saki interrupted me.

"May I have my own room please," she asked quietly.

I was a little upset with what was going on. I didn't know why Saki wanted a different room or why Light was acting so differently. It was very confusing. What could have happened in the hour it took for them to get to the inn? What were they talking about before they came into the inn?

"Yes, ma'am, we have another room right next to their room that I can put you in. For you, it will be 100 yin," the woman said.

Saki reached into her coin bag and pulled out the money and handed it to her, also handed her extra to help pay for our room as well. The woman looked at her weirdly and handed her a golden key. Like that, Saki was gone, making her way up the stairs that was next to the door and vanished. By this point, I was feeling more troubled than normal, like a piece of me was missing. I could have just been desperate for a woman's touch, something I had only imagined in my dreams. Something that was so real for me in the moment I didn't want to lose. With Light's voice, I was reunited with reality.

"Here is the rest for our room," he said as he handed her a purple bill. "Junjie, you need to snap out of it. Everything will be fine in time," he said with a smile.

We received our key and headed up the stairs that felt cold and gloomy without Saki by my side. We came to our door with the number two on it, and I kept staring at the door Saki was behind hidden in the darkness behind the door. I hoped she was all right. Everything was so off tonight. *Light, Saki, what is going on?* I could feel the darkness mixing with the light inside my soul. Before I knew it, I was grasping my sword tightly.

"Junjie, you should let go of your sword," Light said in despair.

When I looked down, I saw a purple mist radiating from the sword into my hand. In shock, I let go of the sword and looked at Light questionably.

"What...what was that just now?" I asked.

"All our swords are tainted with some kind of evil. Mine too. Some of them can help us. Some of them can hurt you in the long run." He paused as he put the key in the door to unlock it. "Your sword is the worst of all, Junjie. It changes your soul if you let it. It

41

feeds on your fear, your worries, your pain, all of your feelings until you change to its will. Your sword will change your heart and how you feel about people and situations. You need to keep that in your mind and heart every time you wield that sword. It takes a part of your soul away," he said as he opened the door and lit the oil lamp by the window.

The room was bigger than I thought. It was going to be about nine hundred square feet, two beds. The walls glittered from the golden paint that trimmed the walls. The designs still were of the tigers on the wall. I looked at the walls for a bit longer than I should have. I was losing my soul, myself, to this sword. How could I stop it? How could I be able to save myself from this curse? I looked at Light, who was sitting, facing away on the bed closest to the window. I watched him rub his face in frustration, like he knew something, no more like he was holding onto something he couldn't tell anyone. I could tell something was wearing down on him, something that was more than just what happened today. A deep, dark sadness he couldn't let go of. If I only knew what I could do to help him through it. Only later would I realize he was trying to help me make the right choices, but I never thought it would be too late to change the future that was forsaking my newfound life.

CHAPTER 6

The Pig and Light's Plan

The next morning, I woke to the sunlight shining in my face. It was a beautiful sight. Ever since I found out what was to come out of my life because of my sword, I had found life a bit brighter once I woke up like myself, feeling normal, with my feelings still being my own. Even though I knew I had to fight the rest of the warriors, I would find a way to keep my soul intact somehow.

I sat up and realized that Light had left the room. He was nowhere to be found. I slowly removed the sheets from my body. The sun radiated off my white skin. I pulled the string out of my hair and felt my hair touch my torso. I could feel it softly touch the middle of my back. I turned to the side of the bed and swung my lags over to touch the floor. I moved my left hand over my face and through my hair, pushed my body up with my right arm till I was standing. I walked slowly to the mirror, which was hanging on the wall next to the door against the right wall. To the left, there was a table that stood to my waist. There was a brush on it. When I looked into the mirror and saw my reflection, I no longer recognized myself. My eyes had become darker. My hair was longer and thicker than before. I grabbed the brush and started to brush through my hair. I continued to look at myself. My chest was bigger, and I had a six-pack. It was completely different from the time I looked at myself in the river. The poor, fragile boy I once was now a man, a man that was fighting for a new world, a better one without people who were trying to kill innocent people, like my family. At that moment, I felt a pain rush through my whole body when I remembered how I killed Saki's father. Yes, he was one of the men who was there when my family was killed, but he also saved my life and got me to this point in my life.

I then wondered how Saki was doing and if she had left yet. Light was carefree and probably went down for a bath in the spring, but Saki, I'd never seen her get to that point where she didn't want to be around us. I put my hair back into a bun and tied the string around it then opened the door.

When I got into the hallway, I looked to the right at the door Saki would be behind. I thought about knocking but decided against it and found myself walking downstairs. When I got to the last step, things seemed different. There was a crowd of people swarmed around this big man. He looked like a sumo wrestler. I saw that all the people around him was staff members. They were holding plates of food, giving this man all the food he could eat. I stood at the bottom of the steps for a moment, just watching. When everyone stepped aside, I saw the mark on his forehead, "Pig," in Chinese characters, glowing in a dim yellow light.

I ran upstairs to grab my sword, but on the last step, I ran into someone and almost fell down the steps. I felt a hand pull hard on my hand and swung me around. I landed on my knees, next to my door. When I looked up, it was Saki wrapped in a towel. Her hair was pulled back and wrapped with a towel. Her face was red. I could feel my nose starting to bleed. I rubbed my nose quickly and stood up.

"Saki…" I said as I looked away from her.

"Manchu… Are you all right?" she questioned.

"Yes, thanks to you," I replied.

"Good. I'm glad. I should be getting back to my room then," she said with no hesitation and left me there silently, with only the memory of how she looked with the towel on.

No matter how bad I wanted to go to Saki, there was a better opportunity waiting for me below—the Pig. The quicker the battle was over, and the less time I held my sword, the better. I was still worried how distant Saki was getting, but I couldn't keep thinking about her when there were so much more at stake.

I made my way to my room. When I walked in, Light was standing by the window, holding my sword out to me. He was looking at me with sad eyes, but we both knew what I must do. I had to. It was my fate to destroy the swords and their wielders. I took the sword from Light's hand. I could feel him shiver. It made a chill go down my spine. I found myself thinking about what I was really doing.

Was it right to kill someone? I mean, I did with my master, but that was the only way to be able to get the sword. There was no other way. That couldn't have been helped. Who was I becoming? What was starting to take over my soul? I could no longer wait. I could feel the pull of the sword, drawing me to the battleground that awaited me.

I walked out the open door, leaving. As I unsheathed my sword, I could feel the power lust of taking a life. The darkness overwhelmed my heart. The feelings I had for Saki were starting to fade. The only thing my soul wanted to hold on to was the pleasure of watching one of the seven fall.

I was losing myself and my feelings as I walked down the steps. The light in my soul was going out the more I was holding on to it. When I reached the bottom step, I was ready to take the revenge that I had chosen to take.

The Pig was still surrounded by the staff, still pigging out on the food they were giving him. I didn't know why they were treating him like a king. I stepped down off the step and saw the fragile woman who had helped us get our rooms last night. She was scurrying across the floor with a plate of food. I heard the Pig yelling for more food. She slipped and crashed. The plate broke, and the food lay scattered on the floor. She sat up, trying to swiftly clean the mess and the glass. For the first time, the crowd broke around the pig. He stood up and started to walk toward her.

This man—no, not a man—a beast of a monster towered over the woman. The inn's ceiling maybe stood ten feet above normal-sized people. This beast's head almost touched the ceiling. He was grossly overweight. His rolls had rolls. His legs would swallow me whole.

His thigh was taller than me. I had to evaluate the situation… Before I had a chance to think of what to do, he grabbed the woman by the neck and lifted her off the ground. Before I knew it, I was running toward him and slicing his hand with my sword, something I would quickly regret. He did drop the woman, but the next thing I felt was his left fist coming to hit me. With the force behind it, my whole body went numb. His fist covered my face, all the way down to my thighs. I flew through the inn's walls and hit a tree outside that stopped me on a dime.

When I hit the ground, I started coughing up blood. My body felt like rubber. My sight was starting to get blurry. I looked behind me to find my sword. It wasn't there. Where could it be? When my eyesight came back, I looked up to hear a loud noise. It was Saki. She was inside the inn. When I saw her, she was jumping through the air at the beast of a Pig. I didn't know why she was doing this till I saw that he had my sword. Saki kicked him in the face. I saw the giant fall from the kick, and my sword went flying. It landed next to the hole in the wall I came out of. Saki ran to the sword. When she bent over and grabbed it, I could feel my heart stop when she stood up. Her green eyes pierced my soul. She stood in the light, looking like a goddess had just come from heaven to help me. Her long brown hair was moving around her like a cure I couldn't break. Her kimono was purple and short; it had flowers embroidered on the fabric. On her arms, she wore half sleeves that went to her wrists. They were tied on her forearm by ribbons. Her smile saved me in that moment. Next thing I knew, she jumped out the hole in the wall and slowly floated to earth next to me.

"So why didn't you ask for help? That warrior is too strong for just you?" she questioned as she handed me my sword and helped me to my feet. "Anyways, where is Light? Shouldn't he be here as well?" she said coldly.

I was in shock, kind of just confused by where she came from and how she got here so quickly to help me, and on top of that one, how was she so powerful? I searched her body, looking for a mark, but no matter where I looked, no glowing zodiac mark.

"May I ask why you're looking me up and down, Manchu?" She looked at me, confused.

"I was…just…" I could feel my face turning red.

"Never mind about that. Here he comes," she said as she got ready to fight.

We both heard a loud, growling noise coming from him as he slammed his monstrous body out of the hole. How made it ten times bigger than it was before. I was struggling to get my air back. I was sure Saki noticed, as she stood in front of me to make sure the Pig wouldn't notice my struggling. I looked around her leg to see what he looked like in the light of day. Since the inn was dark, the only reason I noticed who he was, was because of the glowing mark that lit up his head. He stood about sixteen feet tall. Not going to lie, he reminded me of a sumo wrestler, but he was way more massive than that it looked, as though he weighed a million pounds. It was crazy to think his body could handle that much weight. He wasn't even wearing clothing. It was more like sheets wrapped around his body. The sheets were stained and covered in blood and dirt.

"So it's the little dragon. You finally found me. It's about time. I just don't know how someone as fragile and scrawny as you is supposed to beat me," he roared. His voice was like a drum

His voice was so loud it hurt my ears, but Saki didn't flinch or even move as the ground rumbled under us. She stood motionless, with her arms crossed, looking at him like he had lost his mind.

"One question, Pig!" she yelled. "Do you know how to bathe, or are you scared of water? Your face is covered in dirt and blood, and you smell as though you rolled in a giant pile of cow shit," she said as she stood there, not even glancing back at me to see my reaction.

"How dare you talk to me like that, little girl!" he growled as he started to run forward at her.

In one swift move, Saki and I were in the air. She was holding me close to her chest. I could hear her heart pounding in her chest. I had no idea why she would have said that or acted like that. She was a completely different Saki at that moment, someone I didn't know, the Saki I didn't love. Why would she do that to help someone else? She shouldn't have done that to protect anyone, not even me. I knew I would have just kept my mouth shut and let her take her beating.

This Saki I didn't like at all; she should only care about herself like I did.

In the middle of my thought, Saki stopped in midair. She looked down, with a fierce look on her face, and threw me into the air. When she did that, I saw the Pig had a hold of her leg. He started to swing her into trees and slammed her on the ground.

I was falling to my death. I was sure I punctured a lung. Before I hit the ground, I was caught by Light. Light then turned me to witness the fight. Saki was struggling to get out of his grip. She was still being swung around. She was trying to get into her left sleeve when she finally pulled the ribbon, and her half sleeve came off; she was holding something that sparkled in the light. The Pig yelled out in pain. Saki was free. Her dress was torn, bloody, and full of dirt. Her hair had branches and leaves in it. You could tell that her right arm was broken. She was favoring it even though she used all her strength in that arm to pull out the knife and stab him. We heard a loud rustle coming from where the Pig was at. He was running at Saki again. She jumped up and landed on the Pig's back. She kept stabbing him in the back of the neck. He grabbed her like she was a mere fly and threw her past me and Light. She hit a tree behind us. I looked toward her. I followed the dirt marks to find her sitting on the ground, completely out. Her right arm was pouring out blood. There the bone appeared to be broken on her shoulder. Her face was still so peaceful.

I got up even though it was painful and grabbed the sword I laid beside me when Light caught me. I stood up to face the Pig even though I couldn't breathe, but I must live to finish my task at hand. The Pig finally started to charge at me. I held up my sword, and I realized what his weapon was. It was a ring in his left hand that had a sharp point on it. He swung his left hand at me. I pointed my sword at his throat as he slid toward me. I was waiting for the pain of his weapon to hit me as my sword sliced his throat. I never felt the pain from it. I looked to my right, wondering why. It was Saki… She was holding his hand back while she was getting stabbed on the right side of her torso. If he didn't die soon, Saki would have helped me for no reason, and her death would have been in vain. I swung my sword to finish the job. The Pig bled out and become completely lifeless, and Saki could finally drop his hand on the ground.

Saki turned to look at me. I saw her smile so bright and caring, and as fast as she was there to protect me, she was gone. I didn't know what to think. Saki was gone again. I was alive though; that was the main point. I could live on, knowing I could finish this job. Light stood there, staring at me. I wish I knew what was going through his mind. He looked a little disgusted with me, like he didn't like what was going on. I had to do it. I had to kill the pig, or he would have killed me. I looked down at my sword and realized it was taking the power from the Pig's weapon, and when it got all of it, the weapon and the Pig's body turned to ash at my feet. The people of the town came out of their homes and places of business to thank me for my victory. I looked back to talk to Light, but he was walking away, shaking his head.

Light

When I got back to the room after seeing Junjie take all the credit for destroying the Pig, I couldn't help but think that the sword had already taken the man that was inside the body. My visions were becoming clearer, but still scattered, so I couldn't see how this story was supposed to end as of yet. So many endings, so many choices, and I knew the ending to every ending and every choice. The only ending I could see was Saki's; the ending to my story and Junjie's endings were still unclear because our endings are based on the choices of other people. Saki's future and end was based off of Junjie's actions and choices he made. Now more than ever I needed to change her fate, maybe something not so bad, maybe not the river of blood like I saw. My nightmares were of her death that I had to watch every night. Every time Junjie changed his mind or did something else, it changed, but it was still her death. *Is there any way to stop it at all? Can I save her life without giving up what my weapon is?*

49

CHAPTER 7

A Change in Fate

The next morning, I woke up in the presence of a witch who wanted to heal my injuries for all the good I did for the town the day before. Honestly, Saki never even came to my mind till now.

"So, Manchu, where is the girl who helped you destroy the Pig?" she asked in a soft tone.

"I'm not sure, but I'm sure she is just fine," I said, still with my head full.

"I hope she is okay. Her name is Lady Saki, right? I heard the princess was trying to get revenge on the man who killed her father. I wonder if she will be able to after she finds out it's you, Manchu. She protected you fiercely yesterday without a question. You, though, you didn't even try to help her, not once. Is it because you want her dead?" she said as if she knew something.

"No... Well, maybe..." I replied.

"Maybe you should put down the sword and answer my question, Manchu the Dragon. The dragon isn't something to mess with. It is an evil weapon that will hold your heart. You see that dragon on your sword," she said as she pointed to the gold one on the blade. "It moved there because you are its new victim. It will devour your soul. When the time comes, it will remove itself from the sword and make its new place in place of your soul." She laughed as she finished healing me and disappeared into thin air.

I was so lost. There was so much about this weapon I didn't know, but I guess it made sense. I remembered when I got the sword, and the dragon did come out of his chest on to the sword. I didn't know why I didn't remember that. I set down the sword and decided I would go for a walk, have a clear head, and get away from the one thing that could destroy me the more I thought about it.

I found myself looking for Light. He looked a little sick this morning when he left, telling me he needed some air. Now that I thought about it, he had been looking sicklier every time he woke up. I wondered why that was, and he also seemed to be taking space and time away from me. I also wondered, why didn't he fight with me yesterday? I thought he would always be by my side, but it wasn't him. It was Saki... I remembered how bloody and torn up she was when I saw her taking the injury for me as she held the beast's fist even though her arms were broken.

Out of nowhere, my heart felt a sharp pain. I was worried about her, but why wasn't I worried about her before, not when I had the sword? I was starting to see why no one had ever beaten this sword, and I would lose my soul to it as well. I wondered, though, if my master's soul was taken. *What stopped him from killing me when I was a boy? What made him want to help me? If I think about it, is this even helping, or is it just another problem I have to get through?* All I knew now was that I wanted to find Saki and make sure she was all right. While I was walking, I came upon a path in the woods that went up the side of the mountain, so I thought I'd go up the path and see if I could get a better look of the surrounding areas.

I went through the winding path of stone steps and trees; I was starting to think I had been going through this for a while when I reached the top step, and when I was about to step off, the stone broke from under my feet. I fell through trees. It felt like I hit every tree on the way down. When I finally hit the ground and stopped moving, I could feel a pain under my eye. I took my hand and wiped away a trickle from under my left eye. When I focused on my hand, I saw blood. I must have cut my eye on the way down. The way I landed, I was laying on my back in what I found out to be a bed of flowers. I looked to my left and saw that there were flowers for what looked like miles. I looked to the right, and the flowers ended at an opening. The opening looked like a cave, but it was different. It was made of crystal—a crystal I had never seen before. It shined like a sapphire. The sparkle was magnificent. I decided to get up and investigate the cave further. I rolled over on to my knees and used one of the trees to stand up. When I did, I felt a sharp pain shoot through my leg. I looked down to find I had a small part of a branch that had pierced my calf. I reached down to pull it out, but when I tried, it was way too deep to get out of my leg; the pain was so excruciating I didn't want to move. I realized if I didn't move, I would most likely die here, which wasn't an option. I was starting to wish I had brought my sword with me.

I started to walk slowly toward the opening of the cave. When I had reached it, I thought it would be easy to just be able to walk in and sit. It wasn't that easy. There were stairs that led deeper down into the cave. Luckily, the light from the sun lit up the crystals, which sent the light all the way through the tunnels. The pain was getting worse. The more I walked, it felt as though I could feel a part of the branch scratch my bone and tear my muscles. After yesterday with the Pig, I didn't know how much more pain I could stand. I started to wonder if Saki was worth all this pain. I could have just gone on with my life and finish what I started, with the rest of the swords I needed to collect.

Then the caves started to darken, which only meant the sun was setting. The night was coming, and a little too late for me to get out of the cave. I had no idea how far in I was and how many more stairs I could handle on this leg. I started to sweat. I wasn't sure if it was from the heat in the tunnels or if it was my injury starting to flare up. It might have been starting to get infected, but I couldn't see anymore. The cave was completely dark now. I walked in the dark for what seemed like hours, till I came to a long tunnel. It was long and cold. I saw a light at the end of the corridor. When I got to the end, I walked out into the light. My eyes had to adjust. It was like the sun waking you in the morning when you weren't ready for it to be bright out. I looked around. There were trees and green grass that stood between a path. I followed the path until I came upon a pond in the middle of the shimmering pond. I saw her, Saki.

"Finally," my lips whispered.

Before I could get closer, Saki looked at me with her emerald eyes shining. No hate, no fear, no anger from what I had done resided in her eyes. I felt my heart drop, and only the intense feelings I had for her started to take over my body. Before I knew it, I was naked and beside her, holding her wet, naked body against mine. There was no stopping me or my body now. I leaned in to kiss her lips, so soft and full of love for me.

Saki

When Manchu kissed me, I felt my heart drop. My body was warm all over. He quickly pulled my legs to go around his hips. His touch firm but gentle at the same time. Our lips kept on touching, and our bodies were becoming one heart, one soul, one love that could never be destroyed. I had never felt a love like this before that could fill my heart and fix it at the same time. I could feel the love I had felt for him stronger than ever and hoped he could feel how much I loved him and wanted him in my life. My heart wouldn't stop racing. It was like a drum pounding in my chest, kind of how it always was when I looked at him. I swear we were meant to be together forever. He was silent as I ran my fingers through his hair. His hair was so soft. He smelled so good. I didn't know what it was about how he smelled, but I always noticed it. It was just different now that I was able to be close to him, and his sweet aroma devoured my soul. I couldn't think of anything but giving my whole self to him forever. My love was pure and true no matter what this man put me through. I knew deep down I would always love him, with his flaws. Even when he wouldn't love me one day, I would always love him. His hand kept on caressing my body. I could hear my moans getting louder the more we went on. My grasp was getting tighter on him. Our bodies were so close. Was this a forbidden love, something I couldn't keep in the end, or was it something that would last a lifetime? At this moment, I couldn't care if I would be destroyed. I just wanted him all to myself and to have this moment last forever. Every time I looked at him, his eyes were filled with love. I wondered when

I wouldn't see him look at me that way again. I had a dark past that would haunt me even now, when all I wanted was this man.

When I looked into Junjie's eye, I could see the love he felt for me. When his lips touched my skin, I could feel the passion that I was always searching for inside him. I was nothing more than peaceful. I never wanted to stop looking into those eyes of his. I never wanted this moment to stop.

CHAPTER 8

Rat

Light

"Light?" said a familiar voice from the bar.

When I looked up, it was the innkeeper. She was walking toward me. Suddenly I got a headache. I ended up dropping my glass on the ground. I watched the glass shatter, and through the glass pieces, I saw the new ending for Saki run through the shattered pieces. I saw her and Junjie in the pound of water, the glittering cavern. They were changing her future. Through the beauty of the conception, I finally saw some good, then it changed to a waterfall of blood, and I watched Saki die. Nothing changed the water that was now the color of blood. I sat there, confused, and the pain in my head wasn't helping with the emotions I felt. I could barely breathe. I could feel the pain of her getting stabbed through the chest by a faceless enemy. The person who would end her life was still not certain, so I tried to stand, but the pain in my chest was so painful I was trying to gasp for air. I grabbed a hold of my chest and stumbled to grab a hold of something. I missed the rail and started to fall. When I started to fall, I was caught by the innkeeper. I tried to say thank you when I looked at her, but I couldn't keep my eyes open. Everything went black, and her death just played in my head over and over. The red took over my mind.

I found myself walking next to Junjie. The sky was painted red. The moon hung in the sky, with blood dripping from the moon. Junjie walked silently through the mountains. As we were walking to our battleground to meet with one of the zodiacs, Junjie had the look of death in his eyes. I had never seen before. It sent shivers down my spine. There was an evil pouring out of his aura that night. I was starting to wonder how I had gotten here with Junjie when I thought I had just passed out because of a vision I couldn't handle. Before I had a chance to overthink the situation, Junjie started to speak.

"Light?" he said.

I looked to him, but no good feeling came from me when I looked toward him. His back was toward me because he was walking ahead of me. His voice reminded me of the time I was talking to Amanda—not a women's voice, of course, but as evil as her voice sounded.

"Yes, Junjie?" I replied as I hesitated.

Junjie looked at me, his eyes glowing red, not like the ocean that used to calm his eyes and soul. There were now flames in his soul—a darkness I was worried that would come to pass, the fate I was hoping he would turn from.

"Saki, she has ruined my life, Light…" he said as though he was trying to make himself believe it.

I looked at him, confused, as we stood motionless in the blood that literally poured around us. The more I looked at him, the more uncomfortable I got.

"What do you mean she ruined your life?" I said.

"She's the problem. If she was gone, everything would be better for me and my life," he said.

"What are you talking about? I know you guys have had problems here and there. I don't think you're thinking clearly, Junjie. You love that woman," I said, pleading for him to understand that he was just acting crazy.

"Light, I don't love her. She even knows I don't. I made sure to tell her that. I made sure I told her she was a mistake, and the only reason I wanted anything to do with her was because I was desperate. Light, I never loved her, not once. She thinks I did and can't let me go. She is an idiot to think I could ever love that," he said with hate in his voice.

"Junjie, maybe you should calm down before you make a bigger mistake. You seem to not think clearly when you are mad and just go with the anger you feel. What did she do to make you mad?" I asked, most likely looking at him with concern.

"She's…"

Before he could finish, my head started to pound. I kneeled down to grab my head, hoping the pain would dissipate, but it didn't; it seemed to get worse. When I looked up, I was in a different place. Junjie was gone. I was on a flat dirt ground on top of a hill surrounded by trees. About five hundred feet away from me was, I could see, a man standing in front of Saki. She was on her knees. I saw tears fall from her face. The look of knowing you were going to die settled on her face. She was so upset though. She wasn't begging for her life. She wasn't fighting this at all. What was happening? I looked frantically for Junjie but couldn't find him. I looked back over to Saki. The figure pulled out their sword and without hesitation stabbed her in the chest. Blood splattered everywhere. Her face was covered with splats of blood. The sword was glimmering in the moonlight. I could hear Saki gasping for air. I got up and ran toward her to help her. When I went to put my hand on the hooded figure's shoulder, I fell through a dark hole.

When this happened, I realized even when I was unconscious, I was living the vision. This had never happened before, where I actually could live one of my visions before it happened. Suddenly I stopped falling. I was laying in darkness, lost in the thought of who it could have been. The only person that could come to mind was Amanda. She never wanted Saki to live since she was the one who ended taking everything away from her. As I lay there in darkness, my weapons came to me. My hands felt heavy. I didn't call on these unless I absolutely needed them. It was like they were begging me to use them and fight. I didn't want to become the beast I could be ever again, but I guess I had no choice. I finally stood up and looked down at my hands, the blades shining in the darkness.

My weapon were tiger-claw gauntlets. They were metal boned that went up my arms and around my back for more support. They were like sleeves, heavy sleeves. They never bothered me. I guess it was just something I didn't want to do. I didn't want to fight again. I was so ashamed of what I did with them before I came to be where I was now. I must protect Saki and Junjie now. That's what my weapon was telling me, so I would use them once more until I might rest again. Everything faded to black once more.

When I woke from my sleep, I was laying in my bed at the inn. Junjie and Saki were over me, staring at me. I could feel myself sigh heavily as I turned to the left to look away from them. I wasn't ready to fight again, but I guess I had no choice but to do it again.

"Light, are you okay? You seem as though you have seen a ghost?" Saki said, concerned.

I sat up and looked to Saki and Junjie, who both seemed to have a glow around them, which was nice to see, knowing how Junjie wouldn't look like that in time unless Saki's future changed again. I saw how much they both loved each other and had to try and change their future.

"I'm fine, Saki," I said as I smiled at them.

They both looked at me and smiled. All I could think of was moving onto the next city. So I stood up and ran my fingers through my hair.

Saki and Junjie both stood up with me as I turned to them to say, "Let's get out of here and onto the next battle, okay, guys." I laughed.

Junjie

As we left the inn, Light and Saki stood next to me, and I felt like we would be able to beat anyone as long as we were together. We started on our way down the road through the middle of the town. Now that I got to look at the town a bit more, it was quite quiet and peaceful. There were little shops for armor, weapons, food, and bandages. Luckily, Saki and I went shopping after we were done earlier. I was still wondering how she was healed so fast though; it didn't seem normal. Her wounds were all just scars now, like it didn't just happen the other day. Light seemed to be livelier than he was before. Saki was all smiles. I kept seeing her look at me and smile, blushing a bit. I felt like there was a weight that was lifted off my soul and I had someone I could share it with.

I was happy to have friends, a team I could rely on. No matter what had happened in the past, they were there for me. I didn't want to lose this feeling or run from it, but every time I held this sword, I would get this feeling like nothing else mattered in the world but my revenge. I didn't want my life to be about all the bad in the past, like it had been up to this point. I knew what I had to do, but was it worth losing everything in the process?

As we walked, we came to a hillside. It was breathtaking. The green hillside seemed to go on forever. The trees looked so full of life as the sun fell that night. As it became darker outside, we noticed there was a cabin lit up on the far side of the hill, so we made our way through the field to the cabin, hoping for some place to sleep. With Saki and Light next to me, I wasn't worried. Saki stood closer to me than normal. She was looking at me here and there. I was sure she wanted to say something but didn't. I was wondering what was on her mind after everything that happened. Light got close to me on the right side and looked into the distance. His eye was glowing gold in the moonlit sky. He placed his hand on my chest to stop me from moving.

"Do you see that, Junjie?" he said. I could feel his hand uncontrollably shake.

"No, I don't see anything… Light, are you all right?" I asked, as he looked as though he was trying to hold something back.

"Yes, I'm fine, Junjie," he replied. "There is someone not too far from us I can see them in the bushes ahead. They're watching us." He stepped in front of us.

Then something happened that I never expected from Light. He stood motionless in front of us, then a sudden light shot out around his arms and back. When the light dissipated, I saw something shine around his arms and back. When I got closer, his arms had silver bones that matched his arm bones. The pattern flowed to his shoulder blades. I looked to his hand, where the bones flowed down his fingers, and knives flowed from his fingers that went past his knees. I had never seen Light use his sword. Honestly, I was surprised he had a sword since he

59

wasn't a part of the zodiac anymore. His eyes grew fiercer with every passing moment. He looked as though he was ready to kill. I had never seen Light like this. It was as though he was holding onto something dark. I reached out to Light to try and focus his sights back on us. I was too late. Before I knew it, Light was gone. He was running so fast it was hard to focus on where he was. The only way I could tell where he was at some points was the shine from his swords when the moonlight hit it just right. When he jumped in the air, he was higher than the trees. Saki grabbed my hand, and she started to pull me along as we started in a full sprint. I could tell Saki was worried about what Light might do. I was so lost in what I just witnessed. Light was a badass! I was also wondering why he had never shown his weapon before now.

Light

I could feel the earth around me working with me to get to that stranger. All I could feel right now was, I needed to fight to protect my friends, the only people who were like a family to me. I could hear the moment my swords would brush by a tree and the little ding of the metal when I would scratch a tree. I tried to keep focus because I didn't want to kill something that didn't deserve it. My blades were so sharp they could cut a tree down or a limb off with one slice with very little effort. I was fighting myself because I knew I didn't want to fight anymore, but I needed to, to save Junjie and Saki. I leaped into the air, and when I started to come down to kill the person that was hiding, I saw it was just a little boy. The bright light shined again, and when I hit the ground, I hit pretty hard. I looked around to see where the boy was. I had landed on him. *Damn*, I thought to myself, *this poor kid*. He was out cold. I picked him up in my arms. I heard a rustle behind me. When I looked back, it was Saki and Junjie.

Junjie

When Saki and I finally found Light, he was standing in a well-lit area, his body so firm in place. He turned to look at us. When he did, his eyes had calmed down. They looked sad. His eyes still were glowing in the radiance of the moonlight, but so much sadness was behind them. Saki and I walked up to see what he was holding. I gasped.

"What is it, Junjie?" Light asked.

"This boy is the Rat," I said.

Whatever had happened, the little boy's pants were torn up, and his shirt was torn as well—maybe just came from a poor family. On his knee was the sign of the Rat. When I looked up to Light, he looked like he was going to pass out, like he was extremely sick all of a sudden. His arms went limp. The child fell. Fortunately, Saki caught the child before he hit the ground. She stood up with the boy and looked at Light as he dropped to his knees.

CHAPTER 9

Light's Past

Light sat there, his body limp, hunched over. The moonlight kept shining through his hair. I could see his eyes still shining gold, but this time, there was more sadness than joy. An ocean of sadness had replaced the strong and powerful man that I had always seen in front of me. Saki stood there quietly, with the same look of sadness in her eyes, like she knew what Light was going through. I couldn't help but feel bad for him, but I couldn't show any kind of emotion. Light was my best friend, but I couldn't do anything to help him, not knowing what he was going through. Light looked up to Saki, who was almost in tears now. She nodded and started to walk to the cabin with the boy. Light looked to me next, with a look of pain and betrayal stained on his face. I was confused why he was looking at me that way. He positioned himself so that he was now sitting cross-legged on the ground, facing me.

"Junjie, please sit down. I have a story to tell you about my past that I should have told you before we became so close. It isn't a pretty story, but it needs to be told to maybe help your situation out," he said sternly.

I listened and sat down. I was sure anything Light told me wouldn't change my mind about him. I never really knew much about him. Maybe this could change my mind or my heart about who I kept close. I should stop thinking and listen to what my friend had to say. I looked him in the eyes and was surprised by what I saw. His eyes were no longer gold but glowing silver. It felt like he was searching my soul for answers before he spoke.

"Junjie, this isn't going to be easy to tell you. Do you remember how I told you the cat isn't part of the zodiac anymore?" he questioned me.

"Yes, I remember, Light. What does that…" I paused and realized it had everything to do with it.

He told me it was because of the Rat he lost his spot. That child was the Rat… I could only imagine what Light had to say to me. What he had to tell me about his past, it must be painful for him to talk about. Light was now smiling at me, but only for a moment before he went back to having that same sad look on his face.

"You remembered the Rat is my enemy. Let me tell you why I can't fight him or take his life." He paused and then continued, "Before I met you, Junjie, I was in another group. They called themselves the Black Zodiac. They were fierce, didn't follow any type of rule that this society has for everyone. They would rape, murder, steal, and take what they wanted by force." Light gave a heavy sigh.

"So you would do the same stuff they did, like take advantage of women, steal stuff, and murder innocent people?" I questioned, but I couldn't see him doing any of those.

"I never took advantage of women, not once, even though they tried to get me to. I never stole anything in my life…" Then hesitation caught Light's next words. "I have murdered a lot of people, Junjie, tons. Especially children and women. I have a lot of blood dripping from my hands you cannot see. I can only see it. I never wielded my sword for a reason that blood also stains my blades. I am dangerous, Junjie, even more so with my blades," he said as he looked to the ground.

I wanted to say something, but I knew he wasn't done with his story, so I sat and waited for him to finish. The whole time I couldn't help but think of all the horrible things I had done since I had to take up the sword. I had killed one person I looked up to, just to turn around and fall in love with his daughter.

Light looked back up at me and started again. "I was asked to take care of a woman and her child. So I did what I was told. I stayed with her for months before I was asked to kill her and her five-year-old son. I had fallen in love with both of them. I was so brainwashed I killed them with no questions asked. Only after the fact, I stood over their bodies, crying. I had blood dripping from my blades. That night I told myself I would never kill another person again and put my swords aside to never wield them again. Here I am again with my sword. I don't know if I will be able to control myself."

I felt myself sigh hard and looked to Light. "I have done some pretty bad things as well lately. I am not going to hold it against you, Light. Thank you for being comfortable enough to tell me what you have been through. I am not worried about you losing control." I smiled at him and stood up and reached down to give him my hand. He smiled back and grabbed my hand. Then we made our way, following the path Saki took.

CHAPTER 10

The Road to Fate

Saki slowly walked up to the door of the cabin. The boy she was holding changed to cuddling her and holding her close in his arms. She positioned him to be vertical and moved to knock on the door.

Before she could knock on the door, she heard the boy say, "I love you, Mother..." as he fell back to sleep in her arms.

The man opened the door slowly, and when he saw Saki, he pulled her close to him as he started to cry. She was confused as he pushed her away a bit to look at her. He quickly grabbed his son from her arms. He steadied his son in one arm and grabbed Saki's hand and pulled her in. He let her hand go and took his son through the hallway. Maybe to his bed, she thought. She was now alone in a big room. Saki looked around to see a large table in the middle of the room. She walked into the room and looked to the left and saw a hallway that led to the kitchen. They didn't own very much, but it was a nice cabin. The man came back to the room, almost as silent as a ghost. When he started talking, it made Saki jump.

"Please sit," he said with joy in his voice.

"All right," Saki said, confused, as she sat at the table.

"I never thought I'd see you again," he said as he reached for Saki's hand to hold on to it. "I was so afraid you died in the war, my love." Before Saki could speak, he kissed her.

Saki was shocked. She pushed the man away from her as quickly as possible. The man looked hurt, almost like he was dying inside from her rejection.

"What is wrong with you? The hug was fine. I know you were happy I bought your son back safely, but this is way too much. I'm in love with another man," she said, blushing at the thought of even admitting it to him.

"What do you mean you love someone else? You have been married to me for three years," he said as tears rolled down his cheeks.

Saki stood up. The chair behind her fell to the floor. The noise of the chair hitting the ground broke the silence.

"What the hell are you talking about?" Saki yelled maybe a little too loudly, but not loud enough to wake the boy in the other room.

"Faith, you have been with me. We had our son at an early age, but you loved me. You must have lost your memory during the war." He sighed.

"No, that's the problem. My name is Daichi Sakura, Saki for short. I am and never have been your wife," she said, annoyed.

"Daichi?" he replied. His eyes widened at the name. "You are the daughter of the great Daichi?" His face turned from joy to rage in a matter of seconds.

When Light and I reached the cabin, it looked as though it was only made of logs. The handiwork on this cabin was amazing. We saw a large window where you could see the light of the candles flicker in the night. We walked up to the window, and to my surprise, Saki and this man were embraced in a kiss. The hurt and pain I felt was unbearable. I couldn't believe what I was looking at. She betrayed me. How could she? Light was looking at me with curiosity in his eyes.

"I don't think it's what you think, Junjie," Light said, knowing more than he was willing to let slip.

"She was kissing him. What other proof do I need than that?" I said angrily, not knowing my sword was reacting to my anger.

"Junjie...your sword, it's reacting to your anger. You can't let it devour your soul. If you do, you may do something you will regret in the long run," Light said as he looked to the door.

What Light didn't know was, it was too late.

Light

Junjie slammed the door open. This time, both of Junjie's eyes were burning red. The steam that came off his eyes was most likely the tears he refused to cry. He grabbed Saki and pulled his sword out of the sheath. He slammed Saki to the ground and held his sword to her throat. The mist that surrounded Junjie and Saki became a vivid crimson color. The look in Saki's eyes wasn't fear; it was more of an undying love. She didn't even tremble, not once. Junjie started to let the venom flow from his mouth without another though.

"You are fucking whore, you bitch. That's all you ever were, just some whore that was playing me. I should have known that's all you were. I should kill you for what you did to me," he yelled at her.

Saki slowly tried to get closer to him and touch his face.

"Who said you could get close to me? You're not allowed to touch or get close to me anymore. You're a whore. I should kill you like I did your father! No-good bitch," he spoke.

You could see Saki's heart breaking, not because he wanted to kill her but his words were his weapon, and he knew that. So he wouldn't stop, he knew the only way he could hurt Saki was to distance himself from her. The one thing Junjie didn't know was, she loved him so much what he thought about her meant the world. She didn't care what anyone else thought. The only person that mattered was him. He was destroying her bond with every poisonous word he spoke. I hated seeing Saki so broken, but it might be for the best if they were distant, then the future I saw might never come true. To my surprise, the man started to yell at Junjie.

"It was my fault. I thought she was my wife. She looks just like her! If anyone should die for my mistake, it should be me!" he yelled.

Junjie's grip loosened around Saki as she pulled him off her, not without a cut. She stood over Junjie as he looked up at her. A crimson cut was dripping from her neck. Her hands covered her mouth as everything he said to her ran from her eyes like a waterfall. She stood, gazing at him with no hate in her eyes but a broken soul. If I could choose to see anyone like that, it wouldn't be Saki. She would have been the last person. Around Junjie the mist dissipated as it turned a cold-blue color. Saki turned to me and ran, I could feel the breeze as she passed me. I thought about stopping her. It took almost everything in me to hold back from grabbing her and holding her close, but Junjie had to learn from his mistakes. He might have lost the woman who would love him the most, his twin flame, his other half. I turned my head to the right. I couldn't bear to see her like that. Junjie stood up slowly and sheathed his sword and looked at me like he knew he messed up. There would be no remorse from me from what he had just done. I shook my head, trying to forget, but I couldn't. If she could, that would be a miracle in its own.

"What do you mean she looked like your wife?" Junjie said as he slowly looked over to the man again.

"You told her you killed her father, who was the great Daichi, correct?" he questioned.

"Yes, I did," he said with a sigh.

"His wife, Daichi Sakura, had left him for me. I was shocked such an amazing, powerful woman would want to be with me at all. Before I finish the story, would you both please have a seat?" he questioned.

We both nodded and took a set around the table. Junjie sat across from the man, and I sat to the left of him. I looked at Junjie for only a moment. I saw the chains of fate break their bond, but the other cords remained; their hearts were still connected. Their soul bubbles were still almost touching, and the cord that flowed from the belly button was only detached from Saki, but not enough to shatter them completely. If he chose to fix it, he could. The cords were glowing blue and sparkled in my mind's eye. It was also something I had never seen before. The only way to explain it was, maybe I was getting a new power, not being one of the twelve zodiacs. Maybe that moment I became someone special that could only do what other zodiacs wanted to do. The man cleared his throat, which caught my attention. I looked back at him in confusion, and we both listened to his story.

"Daichi Sakura, she was someone other women wanted to be like. I even looked up to her. she was as beautiful as a rose. She never seemed to age a day; but her husband came across that sword and changed. He was soon forcing himself on her and making her bear his children. Things changed fast for her. I was the friend she could always talk to. She had two children for him before she thought it was best to leave him. Saki was with her dad for a short time before he had to give her up because of the sword's power. When you wield that sword, it wants you to itself and its dark desires. That sword could care less what you want out of life. It only wants its needs heard. Either way, the wielder's dark desires became clear, and it forced that feeling onto you, boy. Just like you almost killing Saki, he almost and probably did kill my wife during the war. She wanted to end the seven most powerful swords. She didn't want children getting killed, women being deflowered by those men anymore. Blood and death are what follow that sword around, and you're letting it get what it wants from you," the man said as he took a deep breath "You do realize you destroyed that woman when you did that, don't you? You didn't even know the truth, and you didn't even ask questions before you were willing to kill her and not trust her. To let you know, son, she pushed me off her. She didn't want that. She loves you or did love you up to that point." He shook his head and looked straight at Junjie, waiting for a reply.

"Yes, I know that, but if she is going to let words turn her away from me, then that's all on her. I don't see how words should hurt someone. They don't hurt me, so everyone should be the same. Verbal abuse is fine to me. If she lets it affect her, it's because she knows it's true about herself, and that's the end of that." He laughed.

We both looked at him with grim looks on our faces. I could see now that the sword might have had complete control of him. Junjie was still there somewhere, but the sword and him needed to be separated for a couple weeks at most. That wasn't the Junjie I came to know and love.

"If that's how you keep thinking, boy, you will get nowhere in life." He stood up from the chair and said, "Follow me. I will show you where you can sleep for the night. By the way, how long has it been since you both have had a real meal?" he asked.

"I think it's been three weeks," I said. "Saki had been eating a little bit more than usual. It was mostly fish, though kind of tired of that. I also think the fish was getting old on Saki too, or maybe she was just sick." I laughed to keep my spirits up.

"Oh, yeah. It makes sense now why she was glowing and so full of beauty," the man said.

"Huh…" Junie and I said at the same time, confused and looking at each other.

"Never mind. You will know soon enough. Good night for now. The two rooms up the stairs you two can have for the night. I'm sure you will want to fight my boy in the morning. Let me forewarn you, he's not as weak as he looks. Also, boy, leave your sword downstairs for the night to clear your head of what you just done." The man disappeared into the darkness.

Junjie listened and left his sword as we went to bed. We decided to use one room for both of us just in case Saki came back in the night. As I laid down to bed, a flash went through my head. It was Saki at the same point when she died again, and the person who was meant to kill her was clear in my mind. Saki's fate was now written in stone. I couldn't stop it anymore. It was going to come to Saki's end. I could feel the tears run down my cheeks.

CHAPTER 11

The Battle Begins

The next morning, I was confused about what happened with Saki and I. It was like a bad dream that played over and over in my head. Light and I were so tired from the night we passed out quickly. I looked to the left and saw Light laying on the floor next to me. The room was a decent size, not to big but big enough for two of us to fit into. There were two small mattresses on the floor that we seemed to find in the night. I turned and laid on my back and stared at the ceiling, wondering why I wanted to laugh and cry at the same time. I had to admit, I felt so much better not having my sword next to my side. Then I remembered I tried to kill Saki last night. I told her I killed her father and I'd kill her the same way. At that moment, I could feel my soul sink inside my chest. I had to see if Saki had come back. I slowly got up off the floor, trying not to wake Light. Little did I know, he was already up.

"You won't find her here," Light said in a cold tone.

"W…what are you talking about? I wasn't looking for anyone. I had to go to the bathroom, that's all," I said as I looked to where Light slept, with his back turned to me.

"I looked for her most of the night. Wherever she is, she isn't here," Light replied like he knew I was lying.

"Well, either way, we should get ready for the fight this morning," I replied.

71

Light turned to me when I said that and sat up.

"We won't be fighting today. Four days from now, we will be," he said as his gold eyes shone in the light that came through the window.

"What! Four days. It can't be that long. We have zodiac warriors to find," I said.

"Junjie, it will be fine. Saki should be back by then," he said as he looked up to me.

I looked at him like I couldn't wait to see Saki, but I knew deep in my soul that I couldn't see her right away after what I did. Light got up and opened the door. He looked at me over his shoulder.

"Let's get this over with," he said with a sigh.

We both walked down the stairs together. We walked into the living room and saw the man sitting at the table with his son. When he saw us, he greeted us with a smile.

The next thing I knew, he extended his hand out to us and said, "My name is Kei Tomi."

Light extended his arm and grabbed his arm and placed his hand into Kei's and said, "My name is Light, and this is Junjie Manchu."

"Nice to meet you, Junjie and Light. By the way, is there a last name to that, Light?"

"Not that anyone needs to know for right now," he said as he looked toward the boy.

"Oh, so I see. My son's name is Tomi Ty," he said as he looked toward his son.

His son ran up to Light and grabbed his hand aggressively.

"Hello, Light, sir, it's nice to meet you," he said with a smile.

Light looked at Ty, not saying a word for a long moment, and then ended up smiling at him and returning the kindness he was given. Knowing Light had always wanted revenge on the Rat and now also knowing his past, how far he had come from where he once was, it would be sad to see him fall once more. My heart hurt for him, but also hurt for Saki and the man I was becoming—someone I could look in the mirror and not recognize anymore. Was I a man or the dragon that consumed me? I watched from the house window as I watched Light and Ty get closer, playing next to the lake, sometimes fishing, at times swimming. I felt the days drag by. Minutes felt like hours, and hours began to feel like days. I overheard Kei talking to Light about waiting for four days to start the fight with his son. Of course, Light cheerfully agreed to the battle then.

Next thing I knew, it was nighttime. Meals began to linger in my mind's eye. Why was I feeling this way? Why couldn't I break the worry that Saki might never come back? That I might never feel the touch of her skin on me? Would I ever be able to see the love that she once had for me in her eyes? Would she really come back like Light said she would, or would she forever be gone out of my life? So many questions, and no one could answer them but for Saki. The only thing that mattered was her now.

Before I knew it, three days had passed, and today was the day Light and Ty would fight each other. The sun was setting in a blood-red sky. I stood, curious if blood would be spilled tonight. The blood that would stain the ground would be unexpected though. How fate had a funny way of working out.

I followed Light as he left the house and made his way to the lake. We were silent for the most part. I couldn't understand why Light was still going to fight Ty that night. They had become so close the last three days they were together. Also, there was something I couldn't shake. Saki still hadn't returned. Did I mess up that bad this time to the point she would never come back? I didn't even know where to start looking for her, or I would have. I clinched the sword at my side. The moonlit sky was beautiful that night. I watched the moonbeam dancing along the water for what seemed like forever. Light was sitting next to a tree, with his eyes closed for a minute before he let out a sigh and stood up. He looked toward an opening in the trees, waiting for something I couldn't hear.

"Are you ready, Junjie?" Light questioned.

"Yes. Are you?" I said, somewhat confused because I wouldn't be fighting tonight, or so I thought.

"Yes, I am, Junjie. No matter what happens tonight, keep your head up and make sure you do what you need to, to survive," he said with a serious tone.

I finally heard some rustling in the forest. Light stood firm. I was wondering what we walked into this time around. Finally, four figures walked into the opening. Two were Kei and his son; the other two I had never seen before. There was a slim woman standing next to Kei. She wore only fur that barely covered anything. Her top was too small for her boobs, so they hung out the top and the bottom of her shirt. He smooth ghostlike skin glimmered in the light from the moon. As I kept on looking at her, I saw she was wearing what looked like undergarments made of fur as well. The underwear looked like it would break off her in an instant if she made the wrong move too quickly. Her hair was matted and looked like she had been rolling in the dirt. Her eyes looked fierce and wild, like a wolf. Her lips were big and luscious. I was honestly surprised her hair looked so bad when she was a good-looking woman.

The man who stood next to Ty was fit. He had muscles popping out of every inch of clothing he had on. He was wearing a kimono though. Looked like he had money. The kimono was not cheap. His face was fierce, and the only way I could think of describing him now was, he was built like a horse. His facial structure was so defined and naturel. For a moment, I thought I was getting jealous of how handsome he looked and for the first time was happy Saki wasn't present. I was happy to hear the woman's voice that got me out of my head just in time.

"Are you the great Junjie Manchu I have heard so much about?" she said. "My name is Koharu Kou. Since you can't see my sign, I will tell you who I am."

My mind was kinda lost in watching her almost-naked breasts bounce in the moonlight.

"Did you hear me, Dragon?" she said in a husky voice that did somewhat remind me of a wolf in plays I saw when I was younger.

"No, I'm sorry. Would you mind putting more clothes on so I could take you seriously?" I replied.

"Junjie, she said she is the wolf from the zodiac, and he is the horse, Yuudia Takeshi. Get your mind off of her body and where it needs to be. This isn't something you should be taking lightly, Junjie.

Our lives are at stake here. These guys aren't like the last people we have faced," Light said. I could hear the frustration in his tone.

I looked at Light and felt my heart drop in my chest. Light knew we were going to fight three of them tonight, but how? There was no way we could beat them on our own. Three against two, and already you could feel the tension grow. I looked up and didn't realize the mutt was so close to me. I could feel her breasts touch my chest. I was only in my head for a moment. I didn't see a weapon, but the thing was, I wasn't looking close enough and knew I was too close to her to escape. She opened her mouth, and I saw them—her fangs. Her teeth was her weapon. The steel from every blade on her teeth shone in the moonlight. I closed my eyes. I didn't know why it wouldn't hurt less, but I did.

I felt something warm splatter across my face. I felt no pain whatsoever, but I could hear her howling in the dark. I opened my eyes and saw the mutt laying on the ground, with blood spewing from her neck. I shot my eyes over to Light, who was smiling for the first time. When he saw my eyes fixated on him, he shook his head no and pointed to a tree that stood behind me. I turned and looked up to where Light was pointing. It was Saki. She did a flip out of the tree and landed on her feet right in front of me. She had a smile on her face. Her eyes were bright. It looked as though her whole body was smiling. It might have been the moonlight, but I could see a light glowing around her like nothing I had ever seen before. She placed her hand on my shoulder and pushed me aside. In her right hand, she held throwing knives. She took her place next to Light. As she did, they both looked at me and smiled.

"It's about time you showed up, Saki," Light said with a smile.

"You know it's always better to make a dramatic entrance." She laughed.

"I think the fight will be more even now," Light said. "Let's go, Junjie." He smiled.

I quickly took my place next to Saki. As I did, I saw a light come from where Light was standing. His tiger claws were back. His eyes had changed color again. Light wasn't a force to be reckoned with. I was happy he was on my side. I swallowed hard and grabbed my sword from its sheath for the first time. The mist had engulfed my whole body. I had never felt so strong before knowing. Was it because I was with the two people I held closest to my heart, the people I trusted more than life itself? When the mist dissipated, I heard Saki gasp. I saw Ty and Yuudai step back. I felt really good.

Light stood with his back away from me, with his tiger claw on his right hand closest to his face and said, "I knew you had it in you, Dragon," as he laughed.

Saki got into her fighting stance, which I thought she looked more like a monkey. One foot would firmly be planted on the ground. Today it was her right leg; the other would be raised just slightly. Her left arm would go up above her head and down like the top of a C, and her left arm would finish the C. She did look beautiful tonight. I watched the breeze blow through her hair. She closed her eyes and felt the wind move through her body. Tonight she was wearing silk pants that would catch the light in the right way. Her shirt was made of silk as well. It was a long sleeve. The sleeves were a little puffy. Around her chest was open more than normal. Her breasts seemed to be a bit bigger than I remembered.

"It's time!" Light said.

When I heard him say that, I squatted down a bit and held my sword in front of me. The first to move was Ty. He was quick. He moved like a ghost. I could barely focus on where he was. He wasn't quick enough. I never saw anything, just felt a breeze across my face, then Light was standing in front of me. I looked to the left and saw Ty rolling on the ground. The dirt was like mist as his body rolled across the ground.

"You are mine, Ty. I am a match for you, not these two," he said as he smiled.

"Oh yeah, Cat, you think you can defeat me," he said as he slowly raised from the ground, with blood coming from his face. "I didn't even feel you touch me. How?" he said, confused, as he wiped away the blood.

"It's called I'm quicker than you, Rat boy." Light smiled, showing his pearly white fangs.

"All right, let's do this then, Light." Ty smiled back.

I saw Light vanish. The only time you knew where they were, were when their weapons crossed each other and the sparks that kept flying around us.

"Well, I guess it's you two against me then. Doesn't seem fair to me. But I'll take you both down," Yuudai said in a harsh, deep voice.

"Let's just hope you can fight and your looks aren't the only thing going for you." Saki laughed.

"You can try. Let's do this. Enough talk," I said.

Like that, Saki and I were together again and ready to fight. Yuudai took his kimono off to reveal thin armor that covered his body. The only reason you didn't know it was his body was because it was shining in the moonlight. If it wasn't for that, I would have thought he was completely naked. It was the same tan tone as his skin. If it was daytime, you could probably never notice it at all. I thought to myself, *Is that his weapon? I never have seen anything like this before.* He ran toward us. Saki must have seen something I didn't, yet she ended up getting out of her stance and quickly pushed me harder than I could ever believe she was capable of. I slid across the ground to the right of Saki till I bumped into a tree. When the dirt clouds dissipated, I saw what Saki was protecting me from. She was dangling about five feet of the ground. Her right shoulder was pitched by invisible spike. I watched the blood drip from spike to spike. There had to be hundreds of them. She was lucky her right arm was all that was hit.

"I got you, little monkey. I'm surprised you moved quick enough to save your dragon though." He laughed.

"I wasn't trying to miss your attack. I was trying to get hit to do this," she said as she ripped the skin that was caught out of the spike.

Her blood drops fell like crystals onto the invisible spikes he had hidden from the sight of my eyes. Yuudai was shocked that she had done that. He was so furious he now wanted to kill her more. As Saki stood in front of him, I saw that he was about to attack her, and I couldn't let her die. I couldn't lose her. Saki stood there, motionless, holding her right arm as the blood poured out from between her fingers. Before I could move, I saw a light twinkle. I saw Light's tiger claws stab through Yuudai, and Ty had come up in front of Yuudai to slit his throat as Light distracted his gaze. As Yuudai fell, we could see the look in his eyes, as he couldn't believe we could beat him. Honestly, I was confused to how Light and Ty would help destroy him together.

"Yes, we did it. Good work, Ty!" Light said as his weapons vanished.

"I know, right. That was so cool. Your plan worked so well," Ty said happily.

"Wait, you guys planned this out?" I said.

"Yes, we did. Light didn't want to kill me, and honestly, I didn't want to kill him either," Ty said.

"So where did Saki go? She looked damaged. If it wasn't for her doing that, destroying him would have been so much harder to do," Light said as he looked around and saw puddles of her blood in the distance.

Light started to walk toward her blood, but I stopped him. I looked at him as I placed my sword back to my side and said softly, "I will go get her."

"All right. I will make camp next to the pound on the far side. Saki and you can meet me there. First, I will get bandages and medicine. Make sure you bring her back. She was losing a lot of blood. She needs to be helped as soon as possible," he said in a concerned tone.

"I will. I promise," I said as I made my way, following the blood marks on the ground.

I walked for a while. I saw something in the distance. It was Saki. I was so happy I had finally found her. I was sure she heard me coming up from behind her because she turned around and smiled at me.

CHAPTER 12

The Broken Heart

When I saw her, all I could think about was how much I loved her but could never tell her about my feelings for her. Saki had told me before that she couldn't fall in love with me unless she could get revenge on the person who killed her father. Saki couldn't now know the man she did love was the one that took her father away.

She was walking toward me slowly, one arm bleeding from the attack and the other reaching out for me. I slowly reached out so I could try to hold Saki in my arms. I wanted to reach out for her, hold her in my arms, and wash all her pain away with my love for her, but I couldn't give her the affection she so desperately wanted. When it came down to it, all I could do was give her my hand so that I could help her along. The look in her face was full of pain and regret. Her eyes were so desolate. She could have made anyone's heart break in an instant. I could never tell her how I felt for her. She wouldn't take me as I was, and I knew that.

as we walked, Saki pulled her hand away aggressively. In shock, I turned to look at her. She was so beautiful as she stood there, strong and so fragile, as the blood continued to run down her arm to her fingertips to the ground, which already was turning crimson. I opened my mouth to speak. Nothing came out. I stared into her eyes. I comprehended that something needed to be said.

"We must get you back to Light so he can help heal your wounds, Saki," I said as I looked in to her fierce but painful eyes.

"Manchu, I can't pretend anymore, the way I feel for you. I told you once that I could love you after revenge. Now that I know you are the one I must kill, I can't. The truth is, I do love you. I always have. I just didn't know how to say it or show you in a way you could understand. I will take you as you are. All the time we had together, even when you saw me naked in the moonlight at the lake." Tears now started to fall like tiny diamonds. "I thought you loved me too. I always try to keep the good memories, not the bad ones, in my heart. Do you not love me, Manchu!" she finally yelled as the sobbing kept on.

"Saki, we are all here for a reason. Mine is to find the zodiac warriors. If you still want to stay by my side, that is your choice," I said coldheartedly as I looked to the ground of crimson. I could tell she had lost a lot of blood, which worried me, so I kept on. "We all have a mission to complete, and feelings of love is a joke in these times of war. You can say you love me, but I know it isn't true. Women can't even keep their thoughts or emotions in check when they need to. There will never be anything between us," I finished, lying about how I felt, and looked up.

She stood there, crying harder than she was before. I knew I tore her heart apart at that instant, but I knew I had to for the future of our country. It seemed like every time all we could do was hurt each other. It just went back and forth, but I knew the moment I looked back up at her, there was no coming back from what I just did. I reached out to touch her left arm because it was the one that wasn't as injured.

She slapped my hand away. Her face reminded me of the way my mother looked at me when she knew she was going to have to leave me, heartbroken, scared, and not knowing what would happen next. Even though Saki had saved me several times, and all the moments we had that were good and bad, all I could think of was myself.

"Listen, Saki…" I tried to speak, but she interrupted.

"Manchu Junjie, you have said enough. I was foolish to open my heart to you. Now I know how you feel for me, and those feelings will never grow. I am pregnant… Remember that night you tried to kill me? I went to a healer to see what was wrong with me, always getting sick for no reason. I have to say goodbye for now. I will not stay by your side, knowing that you have no feelings for me or even feelings about how you will be a father. I'm sorry I kept it from you, but your soul is becoming more corrupt. Even if you do, you will always lie to yourself," she said as she ran off into the forest.

My heart dropped. What did I do? I tried to run after her, but I couldn't seem to move my body. The pain in my body felt so surreal. My heart ached, and my body became numb. I had never felt like this. I thought of her face, her eyes when I told her, watching her tears trickling down her cheeks, her soft hair as it blew in the wind as she ran away at that instant.

I finally gained control of my body and chased after her, but I couldn't seem to find her. I let her into my heart as well, but the one mistake she made now seemed pointless. We seemed to hold foolish things against each other. I had one chance to tell her how I felt, and it was gone in an instant. I lost the person I loved the most because of my pride. I sluggishly walked back to camp, where Light waited for me and Saki to return. But I would be returning alone that night.

I finally made it back to camp, where Light was cooking fish that we caught earlier that day. Light looked back, and when he saw me, he smiled; but his smile quickly changed into a frown.

"Where is Saki? She isn't dead, is she?" he said nervously. "Now that we have the Rat on our side, we should have Saki here with us. I know she is a strong woman who can hold her own, I know that, but I still worry," he said as he slowly turned the fish.

"No, she isn't dead, yet. She couldn't stay by my side anymore." Light noticed the look on my face. "Um… Anyways, she is hurt badly, and I tried to get her to come back so you could help her… She wanted to leave…" I said as I sat down on a log nearby, with my back turned to Light.

"So you didn't tell her you loved her too? She knew you did, the way you two are always ready to be there for one another. Well, she was there for you way more." Light laughed. "She would have died for you. You know that, right, Junjie? She would have done anything for you. All she wanted was your affection. Why couldn't you give her that?"

I couldn't answer him. I was a fool. After everything even, Light knew what I couldn't see. We only had known each other for six months. Could this be true love? Could we be soulmates? Why did my heart feel so empty? The pain I felt inside was more painful than I ever thought it could be. I might never see her again, or when I did, she might be with someone else. For the first time, I realized how much I truly loved her. Now she might never come back. I lost my world in a matter of minutes.

"So I'm guessing you just realized, even when you told her you killed her father, she stood by your side," Light said in an uplifting tone.

"Enough, Light! We need to go to bed..." I snapped, not even thinking.

"Okay, I'm sorry. I didn't mean to hit a nerve. I am with you and will be your support even when you're in the wrong." Light's face turned grim. "Not being one of the twelve zodiacs, though, may be a problem. I am simply the cat who lost his place because of a rat... that I am now friends with... Hmm, who would have figured that? It will be a hard road to travel," he said with a sigh.

I knew what he meant now that Saki was gone... *Never mind that. I can do this on my own, I've... Maybe... I can't give up. Up to this point, I have always had Light and Saki by my side. Also, Saki has helped me with several of the warriors. If it wasn't for her, I could have never beaten the Ox, and she took a hit from the horse so we could finish him off. It's funny how you don't know what you have until it's gone.* I sighed heavily as I tried to go to bed that night.

Meanwhile, Saki had stopped by her sister's home close to the city Light and Junjie would soon enter. Her sister was the healer she was talking about, who told her she was pregnant. She was always there for Saki when she needed help.

Saki

I knocked on the door, hoping she was still awake to bandage my wounds and possibly some stitches.

"Hold on a minute. I will be with you soon," she said.

The door opened, and she saw me bloody, barely able to walk. I was surprised I could even get there, but I guess, when you needed to get away from someone, your body was capable of anything.

"What happened, Saki? Oh my god, I have never seen you this bad, not even with the hit you took from the Ox. I mean, don't get me wrong, that was a bad injury as well," she said as she helped me walk to the table. She sat me down and looked at the cut on my arm. By this point, I could barely move my body. I felt like a motionless corpse just waiting to die.

"Hey, Saki, can you hear me? Saki, I need you to stay awake. Don't close your eyes, Saki!" she yelled.

To me, it sounded like a faraway echo, like she was miles away. I had to say something to let her know I was still there. My eyesight started to fade.

"Cherry, I…" Everything turned to black before I could finish.

I found myself in a dark place. I was floating. I was laying down on my back. I couldn't move even though I was floating. Suddenly a bright light was shining on me. I looked at my arms and legs. I was chained to a table.

"What the hell is going on? Cherry?" I yelled.

I finally found the strength to move. The more I moved, the tighter the bonds would become. The light started to dim, and I started to hear a voice like a whisper next to my ear.

"I will protect you, I promise." It was a male's voice.

When I realized whose voice it was, I couldn't help but cry. I couldn't stop crying. *He isn't here. I'm alone. He has never protected me before…* I knew that was a lie I just wanted to believe it even for a moment. *He can't even be honest with himself and how he feels.* The cuffs that kept me strapped to the table kept tightening. I could start to feel blood in my hand dripping through my fingers. *What do you want from me? Do you want to use me because I make it easy for you? Do you want me to stop caring so much about you? You were desperate, remember. You don't want me or need me. Should I walk away?* I couldn't keep all these feelings inside. They had me trapped. If I didn't ask, I would never know.

If the answer was something I didn't like, I couldn't keep my feelings trapped inside my heart, or I would lose myself. He knew how I felt, but I would never know how he felt and might never know. I thought that was what hurt the most. *Will it make it easier to let him go? To let him be free? I don't need a hero. I don't need someone to be my knight. Then why can't I let him go? Why can't I stop loving him? Even when he treats me like I'm nothing, like a waste of time, like I need to just disappear from his life.* That thought made my heart hurt. If I must let him go. I felt my feelings I had deep inside my heart, somewhere I didn't have to feel the pain anymore. The cuffs opened. I stood up back into the darkness. I saw my sword in front of me, glowing. Instead of being a sword, it changed to a staff. The top of the staff was a huge blade that made its way halfway down the goldenrod. It stood six feet tall. At the bottom of the rod, about twelve inches above the crystal that it stood on, was a monkey holding onto the rod. My sign was now revealed.

When I opened my eyes, there stood Cherry, looking over me. I looked down and found myself naked.

"Why am I naked?" I asked.

"You passed out. I had to cut your kimono off to get to your wounds," she replied.

"Oh, thank you, Cherry for saving me!" I sighed and looked away from her.

"You're welcome, Saki," Cherry said back, bubbly and happy, but then soon realized her sister looked distracted. "Hey, Saki, are you all right? You seem to be distracted?"

"Yeah, I thought I may have lost too much blood to survive," I said as I rubbed the scar that I got from the horse.

"Yes, you did lose a lot of blood, but nothing a master healer like me couldn't handle. You will have to rest a few days before going out, but it seems that those aren't the wounds that are bothering you. It seems like an internal injury," Cherry said in a concerned way. "I know you, Saki. It's something else. I'm here for you if you want to talk about it," Cherry said lovingly.

"It's just inside injuries, nothing that can be done about those," I said as I stood up and grabbed a kimono. "I must just stop letting men into my heart, sister. The first time I thought I could trust someone with it, they destroy it." I laughed.

"I'm so sorry, Saki. I wish I could help you with this pain, but there are even things that I can't heal. All I can say is, it takes time, but I will be here with you to overcome all your obstacles in your way," Cherry said sincerely.

"I can't stay. I have to help with finding the rest of the zodiac warriors," I said with a sigh.

"I'm sorry, Saki. I can't let you go you. Next time, you may not be able to survive a battle of that extant. You would die, dear sister. You have to stay and heal. In three days' time, you can leave. I don't want you to die. Then I won't have anyone left," Cherry said with eyes full of tears. Cherry slowly moved over to me and hugged me, with her body shaking and tears rolling down her cheeks.

"Fine, for you I will stay for three days, but after that, I must leave and continue and find the zodiac," I said as I hugged her back.

"Thank you, Saki. I am really happy you decided to stay. I love you, sister," Cherry said happily.

"I love you too, sister!" I said as I sat down.

CHAPTER 13

Rabbit! Snake!

"Hey, did you sleep well, Junjie?" asked Light.

"No, I didn't sleep at all. I don't know how I'm going to destroy the Snake today," I said with a sigh.

"Well, we are close to the next town, so do you want to start walking?" Light laughed. "Besides, I heard there is a really good healer in the village. We should check it out. What do you think?" he said with a smile.

"I guess we can go see the healer first." I sluggishly got up and grabbed my sword.

Meanwhile, Cherry was making breakfast for Saki and getting her basket ready to go to the herb fields.

"Saki, breakfast is almost done. After we are done eating, I have to go get herbs. Will you be okay to sit at home for a little bit by yourself?" Cherry said.

"Thank you, and yes, I should be fine. You be safe as well," said Saki, questioning her sister's safety.

"I will. I do this every morning for fresh herbs for my medicine, and I always bring a weapon with me in the field just in case something comes," Cherry said happily. Cherry handed Saki the plate and grabbed her basket.

Suddenly there was a loud knock at the door. Saki jumped, not expecting it.

"Hello, we need some herbs and bandages, and everything else that will help with injuries."

"Sister, don't open the door. That's Light, and Manchu is probably with him," Saki said as a shot of pain filled her chest, just saying his name.

Cherry whispered, "Please hide, Saki. I'll take care of them." Cherry yelled, "Be right there," and headed to the door sluggishly, knowing that the man behind the door was the man that Saki loved.

"Okay, but be safe. They are stronger than they look," Saki said as she left to the back room.

Cherry slowly opened the door. "Hello, how can I help you?"

"Yes, hello, my name is Light. This sluggish man over here is Junjie. We needed some stuff to heal up for a battle," Light said with a huge smile.

Junjie looked up at her and was in complete silence; he just stared at her. Cherry smiled back while looking at both her visitors.

"Yes, of course, sir. I have all the bandages you could possibly want, but the herbs and medicine will have to wait till I get back from the field. The freshest ingredients heal you fast." Cherry left the door open and collected the bandages for the two men and walked back to the door with the supplies "Here you go. Is this enough for now?"

"Yes, ma'am, thanks. How much will this be?" Light smiled.

"Is this all you do? I think you are much more than what you come off as," Junjie said questionably.

"It's on me this time. I will have the medicine in an hour for worse wounds. If you can come back in an hour, I will give that to you as well." Cherry smiled. Cherry looked up to the other man, with palms sweating. She was very nervous but kept calm to answer his question.

"Yes, this is all I do for a living. I take care of the people of this town and cure all that ails them. I do nothing else, nothing more, sir," she said with a smile.

"You should be nice to her. She's helping us, man," Light said with a worried look on his face. "We can come back for more later before we go to the Snake's."

"I'm sorry, but I have to head out to get the medicine. If you can meet me here in an hour…" Cherry said nervously.

"Of course, we can. Thank you," said Light.

Cherry slowly shut the door behind. Her she knelt to the floor. Her face was pale, like she saw a ghost. Cherry slowly wrapped her arms around her legs and set her head inside her arms.

"What's wrong, Cherry?" said Saki, concerned.

Cherry slowly lifted her head. "You have feelings for the Dragon of the zodiac," she said in a very shocked voice.

"Um…yeah, he is very sweet, but he can't let stupid things go," said Saki as she sat on the floor, holding her hurt arm.

Cherry looked into her sister's eyes. "There is a problem with this… I…I…might not be able to be with you much longer," Cherry said sadly.

"Why would you not be with me, Cherry?" Saki said sadly.

"I'm the rabbit in the zodiac," Cherry said, almost in a whisper.

"You're the rabbit? Why didn't you tell me sooner?" Saki said in an alarming tone.

"I didn't tell you because I wanted a normal life for our family.,' Cherry said with tear-filled eyes.

"There is no normal for us, and never will be," Saki said as she looked to the ground. "I'm in love with someone I will have to fight in the future. I'm the monkey. One of us will have to die." She sighed heavily.

"It will be okay," Cherry said confidently.

Cherry stood up and walked over to her cabinet and slowly opened it. She reached in and grabbed a whip with nine tails, which was embroidered with razorlike blades going through the length of the tails.

"I'll see you soon. I'm going to the field. I love you, sister," Cherry said with a heavy sigh.

"Be careful. I love you too," said Saki.

Cherry slowly walked to the door and opened it and smiled at Saki. Then shut the door behind her. As Cherry walked to the field, she was thinking about how great it would be to possibly see her sister again. Cherry took her time walking. She spoke with all the people of her village, looked at the sights a little deeper, enjoying every smell, every color she saw. Cherry finally made it to the field and saw the tree where she normally got her herbs. Around it was in a bright spot with long grass and pretty iris flowers growing. She couldn't help but get saddened by this scene.

"Cherry, you will be fine," Cherry said to herself, trying to build confidence in herself to walk over there. Cherry walked slowly over to the tree with her heart racing, knowing that she was a rabbit walking into a trap.

"It's time for you and I to have our fight," said Junjie.

"Why do you have to fight her? Why are we following this poor girl? Oh, you mean she…" Light said with a pause.

Junjie jumped out from behind the bush that him and Light were hiding in and faced the Rabbit.

Cherry's eye's lengthened as she looked at Manchu. Cherry stood there as her soft pink hair blew in the wind and as her sky-blue eyes stared at him as if she was looking into his soul.

"Yes, I am the rabbit you are looking for. My name is Cherry Haylo."

"Yes, it's time for me to destroy the Rabbit. I'm sorry we were put into this because of the past," Junjie said with a sigh.

"Dude, do you really have to fight her? She helped us. We have medicine for when we fight again. Which we would have some leverage in this next fight if you wouldn't have run Saki off." Light sighed as he placed his hands behind his head.

Junjie looked at Light with a devilish look. "I wish you would stop saying that. She is gone, and I don't even know if she is alive… All that blood." He sighed heavily. "Anyways, enough of this. It's time to do this." He pointed the dragon sword toward Cherry.

"Young man, it is impolite to point sharp objects at a woman. Normally, I don't like to fight, but Saki is my sister, and if you hurt her, I will have to defend my family," Cherry said very aggressively.

Cherry grabbed her weapon out of the bow of her kimono. Her eyes turned from a real pretty sky blue to a blood red. Her beautiful pink hair turned white as snow. She brought her arm down and pointed her whip back at Manchu.

"Well, let's do this. I didn't hurt your sister." He sighed.

Junjie got into position to start the first attack. He placed his left foot behind him and his right in front of his body and leaned down and moved the dragon sword that was in his left hand beside the right side of his face. He closed his eyes and sighed. When he opened his eyes, the ocean that once stood in his eyes was now a huge storm. It was like a hurricane in his eyes for the first time. His sword was enraged, but gentler than other times. The flame that covered his dragon was no longer a crimson red. It now fell to a light-blue color—the color of passion from Junjie's heart.

Cherry lifted her arm and jumped into the air. She let her arm swing as hard as she could. The nine tails came swinging down hard into Junjie's direction. Junjie swung his sword in Cherry's direction. A blue flame came from the sword. He felt the pain of the razors pierce his skin. He could feel them in his back and his right arm. The pain from it was almost unbearable. Cherry dodged the flame, but she wasn't fast enough. The flames grazed her kimono and set fire to it as Cherry jumped down, trying to get to the ground. She pulls her whip with her, trying to take Junjie off the ground with all her force. Junjie knew he was in trouble when he felt himself lift off the ground and into the air. The razors dug deeper into his skin. His blood was falling like rubies as he flew through the air. Light was shocked by what he was seeing. He had never seen Junjie's weapon do what it was doing—the blue flame, the storm that was starting to engulf his whole body. It was like watching the ocean take his body, becoming the hurricane that was in his eyes. Cherry quickly took off her kimono and was just standing in her undergarments.

"That was my favorite one. You will pay for that, Dragon," Cherry yelled at him and then started swinging her whip, throwing Junjie from left to right.

Light watched as his friend was being swung side to side, but he had a little crush on her, so he wasn't going to join this fight. Junjie's flames started to make its way down Cherry's whip. The flames roared and changed into a dragon. Cherry dropped her whip and jumped back. When Cherry looked back up, she saw Junjie, bloody and near defeat, as she thought to herself, she could win. A thought came to her mind about how Saki would feel if she destroyed him. Cherry's mind started racing with thoughts of Saki's sad, tearful face as Cherry came home and never being able to see Junjie again. Junjie saw that Cherry was in her thoughts and knew this was a time where he could attack and win. He pulled the razors out of his skin and leaped toward her. He was about to cut her in the shoulder, but something stopped him. He had to look through the flames that had surrounded his body to see what had happened. It was Saki holding an axe-looking rod. The rod was gold, and the blade was wrapped with green gold. His heart dropped, as he saw the zodiac of the monkey on her shoulder. He dropped his sword and kneeled on the ground. Saki stood there motionless for a moment as she noticed her arm had started to bleed again. Junjie started to cry, knowing the fate that laid in front of him and his ex-lover.

"You… You betray me, Saki… How could you do this to me?" he struggled to say through his tears.

Cherry turned around in shock. "Saki, you were supposed to be laying down, resting. You will not get better fighting. You will hurt yourself. Don't fight my fight," Cherry yelled worriedly at Saki.

"I know what I was supposed to do, but I couldn't just let you die either," she replied, looking over her shoulder. "I know what you are thinking, Manchu, but it's not like I had a choice to become this or not. The zodiac chooses who it wants to give its power to," she said in a sad tone.

"No, it's your fault. You knew. You said you loved me, for what? So one of us will have to die in the end. What about the love we made? Was that a lie too?" he questioned, feeling foolish after the things he told her.

Saki stood their speechless. She didn't know what to say for a moment. No, it wasn't a lie. Everything she felt for him was genuine. She loved him more than the air she breathed. He would never believe her, so she couldn't give him an answer he would believe.

"I will give you your medicines if you will leave my village. We have too many people who are going to notice this battle soon. With all the flames and power coming from over here," Cherry said cautiously.

"Deal, we will go. We don't want any more problems for you and your people. It was nice meeting you, Cherry, my white rabbit. My name is Light by the way," Light said with a smile.

Cherry smiled and walked up to Light. "Thank you so much for understanding. I will quickly collect the herbs and get your medicine done. Come with me back to my place so they can have time to themselves." Cherry winked and gave Light a kiss on the cheek.

"Oh, okay, yeah, I will go anywhere with you." He smiled through his blush.

Cherry quickly grabbed her basket and picked her herbs. After she was done, she ran back to Light, grabbed his hand, and pulled him along, running back to her house like they were two kids in love.

"How could you do this to me, Saki?" he asked.

"How could I do this to you? You act like I chose this for myself. Then you act like everything we had ever felt wasn't real," Saki replied, almost in tears.

"Well, the truth is, I never loved you. I just used you, Saki. I was desperate. Haven't you realized that yet? You were easier than I thought to get what I wanted from you," he lied.

"What, even though I feel like you told me this before?" she said as her heart wouldn't stop her eyes from crying once again.

"Yes, it's true. If you weren't around, I would have died several times. When we made love, I was just paying you back for taking all the hits for me. Nothing more," he said as he looked toward the ground so he didn't have to watch her heart break in front of him.

"You were the one playing me all along. How funny. I should have known you can't honestly love anyone. Your heart is so closed off you don't know what you had. You can't see how much I loved you. No woman has ever loved you like I had, and that's what scares you. I hold you higher than even myself, but that's not because I didn't think of myself. Sometimes it was because I wanted you happy, and I was willing to risk everything to make sure you were happy. You are a fool, Manchu! You have made your choice to find someone more worthy of your heart because it's not me. Women that hold others higher than themselves are stronger than most. Even if I was being selfish with you, my love for you is deeper than you knew. I opened my heart to someone who can't appreciate me on a deeper level. You will never know love like I had given you," Saki said harshly as she turned to walk away.

Junjie

I stood in shock as I watched her walk away. The blood kept flowing out of her bandages that were wrapped around her arm. She didn't even show she was in pain or that anything I had just done had affected her in any way. Then why did I feel so horrible for what I had just done? I knew she loved me, and I knew I loved her. *What have I just done?* I lost someone that was more important to me than she would ever know. It was because I never told her how I felt for her. I knew I would regret this moment for the rest of my life. I opened my mouth slightly to try and stop her from leaving me. I saw her look back at me from over her shoulder, her beautiful, fragile body, her long brunette hair blowing into her face and around her body. Her crimson eyes that were filled with water. I watched someone strong change into a weak and damaged woman if only an instant. I could feel her heart break in that one look. I saw her beautiful, full lips open to say something to me. What she had to say made my heart drop. The pain I had felt with those words she uttered to me was like a dagger in the heart.

I watched her disappear. I didn't know what to think. I was so confused. I did love her. She was the mother of my child as well. I didn't know whether to cry or run after her. She wouldn't listen to me even if I did go after her. Even if it was for a moment, I felt the intense pain that she had felt; a woman's heart breaking was more painful than I ever thought it could feel. I knew she was worth it, worth the fight and worth my love. I just messed up big time. I fell to my knees and uncontrollably began to cry. That was when the sword took complete control of my soul. To be honest, it felt good that I didn't have to feel anything, no hurt, no pain. I could move on without her, and she would fall like we wanted.

* * * * *

As Saki was on her way home, she stopped in the forest. She dropped her weapon on the ground before fully breaking out into an uncontrollable breakdown of tears and anger. She fell to the ground and curled up into the fetal position and just let every emotion she had felt out. The pain of Manchu's betrayal was more than she could take. She didn't want to move. She just laid there for what felt like hours, wishing and hoping the pain would go away. It never did…

* * * * *

When I got to the cabin Cherry lived in, I stood outside and leaned against a tree for some time, waiting for Light to come out into the light. I knew that Saki wasn't there. She seemed to travel the other way. Probably needed some time alone, which I wouldn't have blamed her. Because I needed time too. I still couldn't believe she was the monkey I would have to fight later, but the pain of betrayal was what hurt the most. I didn't want to fight her, but at the same time, I felt like it was time to destroy her. I couldn't get my soul to be on the same page. I needed to face that my soul was almost fully engulfed by the sword's power and didn't know what I would be capable of when I was gone from the light and thrust into the darkness. I had only felt it for a moment when I almost killed Saki before, but now it was almost unstoppable.

Light finally emerged from the cabin with a smile on his face. I was wondering why, but he had already told her he had a crush during the fight. When I started thinking about that, all I could remember was Saki stopping me. How much rage filled her eyes and the unpleasant look on her face. Light walked up to me with the bag of medicine he had gotten from Cherry.

"So Saki is the monkey?" he said happily.

"So…she is," I replied.

"That means we don't have to worry about her anymore. She's on our side, so you don't have to fight her," he said, looking at me intensely.

"We do though." I could feel the evil talking for me. "I need her power to become stronger, Light," I said.

"Junjie, you don't need it. It's what the sword wants." He sighed.

"Let's go. We must find the last three that remain, then I will deal with Saki last," I replied.

Light knew there was no way of getting through to me at this point, but the fate he saw for Saki was something he wanted to try and fix before it was too late. He realized now that there was no way of surpassing the power of the sword that would finish taking over my heart soon. He placed the meds in a pouch he must have gotten from Cherry that hung from his side. Light looked back up at me.

"Well, let's head into the city. I believe Cherry said it was a thirty-minute walk from here. The town of Silver Flake. She told me she heard a story of a woman who lives there that protects the town from raiders. She said the stories say she holds a bow that is made of steel. The bow is a sword, isn't that crazy. So she can shoot arrows and destroy enemies with her swordlike bow. She sounds awesome to me," Light said as he started to walk away.

"All right," I said as I followed him.

The sun had already gone down by the time we reached the city. The lights were bright and welcoming as we made our way through the town. We had asked several people about this mysterious woman we had heard so much about. No one would give us an answer, just leads. We started to get hungry, and this was the first time I was able to take a good look at the city. It reminded me of the old Japanese cities; it looked ancient but well-kept together. There were shops that had fruits and meats out in the open. Some of them had outside eating areas. One woman caught my eye. She sat outside at one the restaurants, but the thing that I couldn't ignore was the tattoo of a snake she had on the back of her neck. She sat with her legs crossed, holding a book. On the table next to her was a plate of what looked like beef and broccoli. Next to her plate was a cup of freshly made tea she would sip on occasionally. She had long teal hair and skin that was as white as snow. She was wearing what looked like a halter top. It was a dark-green color that covered everything in the front of her chest; and the straps wrapped around her neck, the straps made an X shape that showed her shoulders, and her shoulder blades off the back of the shirt was completely covering the rest of her back.

The pants she wore were black. They were tight against her thighs. They went all the way to her ankles. She was thin and beautiful in her own way. I had started to walk over to her, and she eyed me with a disgusted look on her face. Her eyes were a sky blue. They looked like viper eyes.

"Excuse me, miss," I said with a little hesitation.

She looked up at me quickly and moved her body away from mine. I could hear her breathing heavily and set down her book. Next thing she did made me jump.

She slammed her head on the table and said in a voice as sweet as a hummingbird, "Two more please." You could hear the irritation in her voice.

I watched as the man scurred around and grabbed two more cups of tea and set them down two sets down from where she sat. Light walked over and sat down where one of the cups sat. I was so confused. She seemed to not want anything to do with us at all, but at the same time, she wanted us to sit.

"Thank you for inviting us to sit," Light said with a smile.

"You're welcome," she said warmly to Light.

"My name is Light. May I know your name, ma'am?" he said cheerfully.

"My name is Viper Lee." She smiled.

"Nice to meet you, Viper," Light said.

"Just Lee to you," she hissed.

"All right, Lee. Nice to meet you," he said as he sipped the tea.

I sat down in the chair closest to her. There was one seat empty between us. I started to sip the tea. I was about to say something, but she rang in first.

"What can I do for the great Dragon?" She sounded more annoyed.

"Do you have something against me?" I replied.

"Well, since you brought it up, I'm not interested in someone who can't lead and can't take control of their own weapon," she said, not even looking at me. "You are a pathetic fool. I can smell the negative energy flowing off of you." She said this more cheerfully.

"How did..." I started to say.

"How did I know that you only want blood." She sighed as she reached down and picked up a baby blue viper from the ground.

"Yes…" I said, trying to not get any closer.

"Does she scare you?" she questioned.

"I don't like snakes much," I replied.

"Don't worry. She only kills what I ask her to. You seem like you want to lose a lot in your life. Your name is Junjie…huh?" she said without pausing more. "She told me what your name is and has told me a lot about your travels…also the love you choose to lose."

"The snake?" I said abruptly.

"Yes, I had her follow you for some time. Also, the snake's name is Sky," she said as she rolled her eyes at me. "Junjie, I have heard that Light has been trying to get you to see what you are doing to yourself. Your last battle was a shock, wasn't it? You were finally able to get some of your powers, the flame of the dragon. Did you know you could use that?" she said, this time staring at me. I felt like I could feel her eyes looking through me.

"No, I didn't know I could do that at all. Is it possible I could have more power than that?" I questioned.

"Yes, but the problem is, you can't achieve it anymore. Revenge and hatred were your downfall, Junjie," she said as she laughed.

"What are you even talking about?" I asked.

"Light has been trying to tell you the whole time, just in the nice way," she said, this time looking at Light, and Light looked back at her. "Light, you can't be nice to someone who thinks they know everything there is to know." She looked back at me. I could feel myself swallow hard. "You are a fool because of what you have done, such as the twelve of us. I am surprised you found the thirteenth, the Cat, first. Luck was truly on your side, having him with you first. You ignored it all though. If you keep going through life thinking you know everything, you will fall and fall hard," she said as she laughed.

"Can you just get to the point?" I said, irritated now.

"You needed all twelve to reach your true power." She laughed harder now.

"Yes, when I kill them, I gain their power. That's what I've been doing," I replied.

"No, dummy, your sword does. You gain nothing. You are helping your sword gain the power, which makes it easier for it to control you, but don't worry. In a couple of days you, will be freed from the sword's control, but at what cost to you…I wonder?" she said, this time looking serious.

"This whole time I have been collecting the twelve swords. I was supposed to collect the seven strongest," I said as I looked down at my cup of tea.

"Yes, I get that, but you interpreted it wrong. Did you ever wonder why there was only seven warriors who killed your family? It's because the last owner of that sword killed everyone else. The zodiac has been trying to fix his mistake for the last century. Right now, I could kill you without lifting a finger. You are no match for me, not now. I will not follow a coward. Also, know that you have killed most of the warriors. Not saying that that is any fault of your own, but since you can't gather the twelve, you will never have the power you need. Yes, collect us, not destroy us," she said.

This whole time Light was trying to convince me to do what he did with the Rat: make friends with them and keep them close. Thanks to Light and Saki, I could control it more, but now. I had nothing and couldn't even gain my full power.

"Honestly, I think the Dragon finally got it. You can take off that crown now, Junjie. You are in trouble when you meet the last two of the zodiac. They have tapped into their full potential, something you won't have till you turn the last page," she said as she drank the rest of her tea and stood up.

She started to walk away, with her snake wrapped around her wrist. Her hair was almost down to her butt. I watched it sway back and forth as she walked. She quickly looked over her shoulder and glanced at me.

"Your last battle will be up there," she said as she pointed to the top of a hillside, where a large castle-like building stood. "They are already there, waiting for you. I wish you luck because you're going to need it," she said as she turned away and kept on walking.

As she walked away, I could hear her yell, "I'm going to finish my book. Let me know who wins."

I was so confused by her. She knew so much. Also, what did she mean by, I would soon be freed from my sword? What else was I about to do that I wouldn't have control to stop myself from doing? Fear was known deep within me. What was it? I needed to know, but the last battle was just before me. I looked over to Light, who sat on my left side. He glanced up at me slightly.

"It's time, Junjie. Let's go," Light said as he stood up.

I followed behind him slowly as we started up the path, the one I might never come back from. It was time for an end, or a new beginning. I was about to find out.

CHAPTER 14

The Prophecy Fulfilled

Light

The sky was painted red. The moon hung in the sky, with blood dripping from the moon. Junjie walked silently through the mountains as we were walking to our battleground to meet with the last of the zodiac. Junjie had the look of death in his eyes. I had never seen before. It sent shivers down my spine. There was an evil pouring out of his aura that night. I was starting to wonder how I had gotten here with Junjie when I thought I had just passed out because of a vision I couldn't handle. Before I had a chance to overthink the situation, Junjie started to speak.

"Light?" he said.

I looked to him, but no good feeling came from me when I looked toward him. His back was toward me because he was walking ahead of me. His voice reminded me of the time I was talking to Amanda—not a women's voice, of course, but as evil as her voice sounded.

"Yes, Junjie?" I replied as I hesitated.

Junjie looked at me, his eyes glowing red, not like the ocean that used to calm his eyes and soul. There were now flames in his soul. A darkness I was worried that would come to pass, the fate I was hoping he would turn from.

"Saki, she has ruined my life, Light…" he said as though he was trying to make himself believe it.

I looked at him, confused, as we stood motionless in the blood that literally poured around us. The more I looked at him, the more uncomfortable I got.

"What do you mean she ruined your life?" I spoke.

"She's the problem. If she was gone, everything would be better for me and my life," he said.

"What are you talking about? I know you guys have had problems here and there. I don't think you're thinking clearly, Junjie. You love that woman," I said, pleading for him to understand that he was just acting crazy.

"Light, I don't love her. She even knows I don't. I made sure to tell her that. I made sure I told her she was a mistake and the only reason I wanted anything to do with her was because I was desperate. Light, I never loved her, not once. She thinks I did and can't let me go. She is an idiot to think I could ever love that," he said with hate in his voice.

"Junjie, maybe you should calm down before you make a bigger mistake. You seem to not think clearly when you are mad and just go with the anger you feel. What did she do to make you mad?" I asked, most likely looking at him with concern.

"She doesn't trust me. She didn't even want to tell me she was pregnant. If she has this baby, it will end up destroying everything I have been trying to build," he spoke.

"Wow! Wait… What? She's pregnant?" My mind was blown. I never expected that. "That's a good thing, don't you think. It shows how much you want to be with each other," I spoke.

"No, I don't want to be with her. I'm good alone. I like it that way. No more problems or her hanging over my head," he said, getting madder.

"Junjie, you need to think about how you really feel and not let that sword take control," I said as he turned to look at me.

Junjie was holding the sword tightly in his grasp. At that point, I knew it was too late, but at the same time, I knew there was no way I could stop him. My new vision, the one that killed me the most inside, was coming true. All I could do look at him. Everything was all over now. The last year we have traveled together, and not once did he ever stop to listen to me. The only thing I could think at this point was, *I'm sorry, Saki. I tried.*

"Light, I will finish the last two off, then I'm going after Saki," he said with a serious tone.

I just nodded. We continued our walk to the castle gates. The gates looked like they were made of steel. They must have stood twenty feet tall. I could be overexaggerating a little, but they were tall. Junjie reached out to touch the gate, but before he did, they started to open. We saw three figures start to walk up from the castle doors.

Everything seemed to be painted red in my mind. There was no coming back from this. I could feel it deep inside. No matter how much I have seen and done on this adventure, at least I had my full power even if I wasn't a real zodiac warrior. Junjie didn't. All he had was the dark power of his sword, which wasn't as powerful. I prayed for a miracle.

We only had three more to fight: the Rooster, Tiger, and Goat. Not having Saki here to fight made us outnumbered. There was a tall woman standing in the middle of two men. She was wearing a short-cut dress that showed off her huge boobs. *Why do some of these women dress so skimpy?* I thought. I shook my head and got back on track.

Her skirt was so short you could almost see everything. Luckily, she wore tiny shorts underneath. She had long black hair that was pulled into a ponytail at the top of her head, but her hair still almost touched the ground as she walked. She was wielding a hammer-looking thing. It was bigger than her. I was surprised she could carry it without breaking. She was so skinny.

Next in line to the left was a tall man. He was wielding a smith. It was longer than one of his arms. He kept on swinging it back and forth. He had muscles that popped out of every inch of his clothing. He looked like a bodybuilder. His hair was short and brown and looked really soft. He had a smile on his face that showed his fangs. He was the one we had to watch out for. I looked to the right of the women. There was a... Wait, where did the nerdy-looking guy go? Nobody seemed to see him disappear but for me at this moment.

I looked over to Junjie. The sword was trying to take him over completely now. I could see him shaking, and as he removed the sword from its sheath, the red mist took him over. I stared at the mist tornado around Junjie.

When it dissipated, the person who stood there looked like Junjie, but he wasn't himself. His eyes looked like dragon eyes. There were dragon scales covering his forehead and around his ears. His hands looked like claws. I was about to say something, and Junjie lapped after the Tiger, which left me with the prostitute. I felt my eyes roll.

I ran in the direction of the woman. As I did, my tiger claws appeared before I attacked. She put her well-polished finger in my face to ask for a moment. I almost fell when I was stopping. I stood there for what seemed like forever as she fixed her hair and put more makeup on her already made-up face. Finally, she looked at me and spoke.

"My name is Marie Rose," she spoke.

I could feel myself dying inside, but I wasn't going to show her the pain she made me feel waiting on her. I didn't answer, just attacked her. When I did, she stopped my claws with her hammer. I was surprised she moved so quickly with such a huge weapon.

"Can't you give me your name, Cat?" she said sharply in a harsh tone.

"Light. Nice to meet you," I said as I jumped over her and did a backflip.

I landed on my feet. I looked at her as I rushed for another attack. This time, I cut her on her shoulder, but she had also hit me in the side with her hammer, which made me fly into the castle wall. I was laying on the ground, watching Junjie for a moment. He seemed to be using a new attack. It looked like a tornado of fire. The tiger seemed to be able to cut down all his attacks, and Junjie was in a bad way. I could see his blood getting spilled, but it didn't seem to faze him. He kept attacking without resting a moment. It was nonstop attacks. I stood up and realized I needed to help Junjie before he died.

"Awe, poor kitty... Did that hurt?" she questioned.

"Not as much as this will hurt you," I spoke.

I had an attack I hadn't used in a while but desired to know that I needed to. I placed my fists to my side and felt the electricity flowing through my body. I moved my hand out to attack and watched the bolts dance through my claws. I looked at her. It didn't seem like she knew her special ability yet. I thought to myself, *Don't kill her unless you have to.*

I ran at her as fast as I could. She wasn't expecting my speed, so her reaction was too slow. When I got to her, I jumped in the air and came down on top of her, striking her in the left shoulder and on the right in her stomach. I watched the electricity flow through her body as I pulled my claws out. They might have been soaked in blood once again, but she wasn't dead.

I stood up and ran to Junjie's side. I got there in the nick of time. My tiger claws radiated so bright when I blocked the tiger's attack. He looked stunned. I could hear Junjie gasping for air, but the sword wouldn't let him rest. I thought I had the Tiger with my lightning bolt, or at least it would stun him for a moment, but it didn't.

He moved so quickly I missed his next move. I thought he was going for the left, so I blocked the left side, then I felt a pain from the right as his weapon dug into my lag. He then grabbed me by the hair and threw me halfway across the courtyard. Something needed to change. Junjie needed help. The next hit would kill him. I heard a cry in pain come from Junjie's direction. I looked up and saw that Saki took the next hit for Junjie. Her right side was soaked in blood as she held his weapon with hers, their blades sparking as she held him off.

At that moment, Junjie jumped up, his sword engulfed in flames, and came down and cut off the Tiger's head. I saw Saki fall to one knee as her weapon hit the ground. She was holding her side. Junjie walked up to Saki with an icy, cold stare. I got up and stumbled as I made my way to Saki. I saw this before. *Saki, I'm coming please.* I couldn't get there fast enough. Junjie had stabbed Saki through the chest. I watched as she let him. I screamed at the top of my lungs.

"Saki! No!" Tears ran down my cheeks.

Saki

I stood, looking at Junjie, as I held my side, trying to make the pain of the cut go away. When he stood over me, he looked so cold.

The Junjie I loved was no longer inside him. I picked up my rod so I could try to get back on my feet. I stood in front of him, about to reach out for him. At that moment, I felt the cold steel of his blade pierce my chest. I felt tears start to fall from my eyes.

Junjie

The volcano of venom that spread through my body as I heard her gasp for air. I heard her dying words escape from her lips.

"I love you."

How could she love me? A beast that ripped her and her child's life from her. When her rod hit the ground, it evaporated into tiny bubbles that sparkled and shone like stars in the night sky. It didn't become a part of me and my sword; it just dissipated, like her life.

When I came out of the evil that had me trapped in the depth of darkness, I looked at my hands that were now blood-soaked. Where did the blood come from? I saw Saki lying motionless on the ground and realized what I just did. The woman I once loved was laying on a blood-soaked ground. I tried, but I couldn't stop myself from crying uncontrollably. Light was behind me. He looked sick, stunned, and shocked at what I did. Light's eyes showed more than words could say. He brought to reality what I was thinking. I murdered her and our child for what power, when I had what I wanted in front of me the whole time and didn't realize it. Light handed me the medicine and then grabbed Saki's body.

"I will bring her body to Cherry. She needs to be with family," he said, eyes full of tears.

I couldn't move, frozen in time. *What have I just done?*

BLACK ZODIAC

The air was thick. I could feel my lungs starting to throb with pain of the icy air I was breathing in. It was too dark to see where I was walking. The pain made it almost impossible to move. Every time I tried to move, it was like a knife stabbing me all over. I was hoping the pain would subside soon. My hands felt warm, and something like liquid was dripping from them. I could feel the ice-cold grass in my hands.

Finally, the pain started to slowly get better. I could finally sit up. When I did, something started to form in the distance. What was it? It started off blurry and out of focus. What was going on? As it slowly came in to focus, I saw two silhouettes fighting each other. This seemed familiar for some reason. At that moment, I felt a sharp pain pierce my heart. The pain was so excruciating I almost fell back to the ground.

I found the strength to stand. I felt my arm quickly grab the left side of my chest. The closer I got to them, the worse the pain was getting. Then I saw it. I didn't know how to react. *Why? Why!*

My eyes were full of rage as I attacked Saki. What was I doing? Why did I... I fell to my knees and started to cry. I covered my face with my hands as I started to cry. I felt the warm substance drip on my face. I jolted and saw my hands were covered in blood.

I sluggishly looked to the ground as I did. I was sitting in a puddle of blood as I sat there in shock. I was thrown to a nice, sunny day. I was dizzy from the force that was behind the jolt that was throwing me around. I saw a minka. It was beautiful.

I saw a little blonde girl, maybe the age of ten, running up to me. When she got to me, that was when I noticed the ball at my feet. She looked up at me for a moment, but those eyes. Her eyes were a bright blue mixed with teal. Her face looked so much like Saki's. Her hair was long, maybe to the center of her back. I watched as she looked back at a stranger, but she seemed to be comfortable with him. I wanted to keep my eyes focused on this beautiful little girl. He said her name.

"Himari, let's see how your mother feels today," the strange man said with a smile.

His hair was brown. He stood about five feet eight inches. His eyes were a deep crimson color, but very stunning. I found myself following them into a dark room, with a bed in the middle of the room. I saw a woman lying in the bed, moaning in pain. I saw a leg come to the side of the bed to sit. I couldn't see her face no matter how much I tried. I saw a deep scar on her side, almost like a burn, then I saw a scar on the left side of her chest. Then I heard the little girl yell from outside the closed door, where the little bit of light shined in, so I could see the healed wounds on this woman's body.

"Mommy? Are you feeling better?" she yelled in a cute, sweet, but soft voice.

Then I heard a name I hadn't heard in ten years that made my heart stop and my eyes water.

"Saki, my love, is you ready to get going?" the man said.

Could it be true? She stood up and wrapped her naked body with a robe and stepped toward the door. As she opened the door, the light filled the room with light. As I watched her, she looked back, and I saw her.

"Saki? I'm so sorry," I whispered under my breath.

The light was becoming brighter, almost blinding. I jumped right out of my bed and hit the floor. When I realized it was all a dream, I was soaked in sweat. I sat up slowly and rested my body on the side of my bed and sighed heavily and started to cry.

CHAPTER 1

The New Beginning

I woke up the next morning to a banging on my cabin door. I didn't want to get up. I wanted to just sit there and let the days pass me by like I did so many of them before. I looked to the left and saw my sword leaning against the wall, where it had stayed for the last couple of years. I had a deep fear, if I had to use it again, I'd hurt someone else. The banging at the door started getting louder, or it might have just been my pounding headache I had. I tried to ignore the door, but I wouldn't be able to do it forever. Disappearing was harder than I thought, especially from Light.

"Junjie. Hey, it's me, Light. Open up," he yelled.

"I don't want to right now, Light. I'm still resting. I had a long night," I said as I struggled to get up off the floor.

"Lee found out some information you would like to hear. It's not good news, Junjie. You're not going to like it. We may have to pick up our weapons and fight again. Can you hurry up? I don't keep talking to you through the door," he said, sounding frustrated.

I felt my heart drop. I must carry the dragon sword again. *What if I go mad again? I know, I don't want that again. On top of that, how are we supposed to do that? I killed all the members when I went crazy for power. There is me, Cherry, Light, Lee, and Ty. How the hell are we going to be able to do anything?* I froze in fear of not knowing.

"Light, go away." My voice trembled.

"Uh, well, we need to talk, so meet Lee and I at my house around noon. Please. You will be interested in what she has to say," Light said, frustrated, as I could hear him walk away.

I stood up slowly and sat on my bed, confused on what I needed to do. I mean, I knew what I needed to do. I just wasn't sure I could do it. I had so many questions, but did I really want to know the answers to these questions? I had faith in my team, but Lee hated me and wouldn't work with me, so could I even say we were a team?

I didn't even know what she could do or how powerful she was. I'd never seen her fight before. Our last battle, if she would have helped, would it have made a difference? Could she have saved Saki if I wasn't so weak? If anyone deserved to die that day, it was me, not her. I often wondered how life would have been with her and my unborn child if I didn't get taken over by the darkness in my soul.

I was so mean to her there at the end of everything. I wondered if she even knew how I felt about her. I should have told her how I felt about her, held her close longer, and made her laugh instead of letting her feel pain. I regretted it so much.

I was alive though, and I must keep pushing through the pain. I must do what I could for everyone else, not just sit here and feel sorry for myself. I took a deep breath and let out a giant sigh. I stood up and walked outside to the lake that was outside my cabin. Looked into the water and saw my reflection.

What kind of man do I want to be now that I can control myself? I took off my robe and jumped into the lake. I washed up and got out. My long blond hair was to the mid of my back. I looked at it and thought maybe I should cut it short like Light's. As I thought about it, I looked around, and my eyes stopped at my master's grave.

I put my white robe back over my body and walked over to his grave. I stood over it for a moment, and then I looked at the road, remembering how this whole thing started and our fight that ended his life. Then the horrible flash of me killing Saki crept in like a nightmare.

"I'm sorry, Master. I failed you, and in doing so, I killed your daughter and my only love. Why does the innocent have to die to make a change in the world? I wish there was a way to not have to destroy everyone's life to make a difference. I promise if I can make a difference in someone else's life this time. I will," I said as I turned to go back to the cabin and cut my hair.

"It's time for a change, Light. I will be there at noon to see you and Lee," I said with confidence.

I started making my way to Light's and Cherry's home in my hanfu. It was black, with white dragons embroidered on them. It was nice to feel like a new person, new short haircut, and it had been a long time since I dressed so nicely. I was finally feeling like I could do more, and I felt confident for the first time in years. I griped my dragon sword and pulled it from the sheath.

Before my very eyes, my sword was covered in a blinding light. When the light died down, my sword was see-through and was sparkling like a diamond. The blade became a dragon itself and was purified completely. My heart sank, and I knew at that moment, this happened because of Saki's sacrifice for my soul. She loved me so much her life was what she gave up for me.

I sheathed my sword. I looked up and saw the entrance to the town. The sign over the town said, "Welcome to the town of Silverton." The town had changed a lot since I last saw it, the buildings looked a lot fancier, and the town seemed bigger. There were a lot more tourists shopping in all the small shops around town.

It was hard to walk through everyone. It was so packed. I was hoping no one recognized me as I walked through the town. Suddenly the crowed broke, and there was easy access on the street. I had no idea what was going on. All the people stood out of the street and to the side of the shops. As I looked around, I was the only one on the street.

I looked at all the strangers' faces and realized they looked terrified. I was confused. Was it me they were so afraid of? I didn't think there was any way they could realize I was the dragon warrior since I changed my whole appearance. I kept looking around for someone else they could be afraid of or if there was trouble in the town. Suddenly I heard someone scream. I ran in the direction I heard the scream come from. I ran to a dark alleyway and heard a woman in the dark, yelling.

"Please don't. Leave me alone!" yelled the woman's voice.

"I do what I want, and you will give me your body if that's what I want, woman," a male's voice growled back.

"No!" she screamed as I heard clothing get ripped.

"Excuse me, sir, leave the woman alone," I said as I struggled to see the hooded figure.

"Blondie, you should leave. This is none of your business," he spoke.

"I'm sorry. I can't just stand by and let this happen to one of the people in this town," I spoke.

I heard a movement of some sort. I never heard a nose like this before, but I knew I had to move before it came closer. I jumped out of the way and landed on a building that wasn't too far from me. I was confused as I watched an energy fly out of the alley. It was a yellowish color. I'd never seen an energy attack look like that.

It looked like there were several black lightning bolts coming off it, and the energy was very powerful. I jumped off the building and back into the street. The woman ran out of the alley, screaming. Her dress was ripped from the bottom up to her crotch. *What the hell is going on here?* I thought to myself. Then I remembered what Light told me about this organization, the Black Zodiac.

"Junjie, this isn't going to be easy to tell you. Do you remember how I told you the cat isn't part of the zodiac anymore?" he questioned me.

"Yes, I remember, Light. What does that..." I paused and realized.

It has everything to do with it. He told me it was because of the Rat he lost his spot. That child was the Rat... I could only imagine what Light had to say to me. What he had to tell me about his past, it must be painful for him to talk about. Light was now smiling at me, but only for a moment before he went back to having that same sad look on his face.

"You remembered the Rat is my enemy. Let me tell you why I can't fight him or take his life." He paused and then continued, "Before I met you, Junjie, I was in another group. They called themselves the Black Zodiac. They were fierce. Didn't follow any type of rule that this society has for everyone. They would rape, murder, steal, and take what they wanted by force." Light gave a heavy sigh.

"So you would do the same stuff they did, like take advantage of women, steal stuff, and murder innocent people?" I questioned, but I couldn't see him doing any of those.

"I never took advantage of women, not once, even though they tried to get me to. I never stole anything in my life…" Then hesitation caught Light's next words. "I have murdered a lot of people, Junjie, tons, especially children and women. I have a lot of blood dripping from my hands you cannot see. I can only see it. I never wielded my sword for a reason that blood also stains my blades. I am dangerous, Junjie, even more so with my blades," he said as he looked to the ground.

I was busy in thought. The man in the hood came out of the alley. His head was still covered. I couldn't see his face. I stepped into something I couldn't step out on now, so I was going to have to try and finish this if I could. I stood there, staring at this figure, waiting for something to happen, but he just stood there, motionless.

"Are you going to take off the hood, or am I just going to be standing here, staring at a hood, waiting for something to happen?" I said. I was curious of what this person looked like.

At this point, everyone in town was running around, frantically trying to find a place to hide. *These poor people have been so tormented by these people, and I stayed in hiding, feeling bad for myself instead of saving this town. I am here now, and I will do something about it.* I grabbed ahold of my sword, and that was when he took his hood off and slammed a large axe/hammer-looking weapon on the ground.

I knew it was heavy. It made the ground shake. It looked like it was made of gold or rare iron. It was round and bulky on the back side of it. The blade was longer than his arm, and thin. It was shaped in an S. It had a gem all over it to make it look clumpy and like wood, maybe tiger eye, if I had to guess.

He threw his hooded cap from his body; I finally saw him for the first time. He was bigger than he looked when he had the hood on. I was taken back from the look of him. His arms were swollen, like a full-grown tree's trunk. His legs were about the same. I started to wonder what I got myself into. His head was big as well. He had thick black, greasy hair that was pulled back into a bun at the top of his head. His eyes were black as a night sky with no stars in the sky. He had a half mask of a bull, was what it looked like. It had small horns on the top of the mask that were glowing red. His mouth was long and slim. His grin was mischievous and could send shivers down anyone's spine. He wasn't wearing a shirt, but his bottoms were torn and covered in fur that had a tail. His pecks were huge, and I could see his six-pack busting off his body. You could see the sweat droplets start to form, hanging from the back. His shoes were black and made him look like a bull. We stood, looking at each other for what seemed like forever, till he finally started talking.

"You little man, you should have known better than to interfere with my business," he said in a deep voice that rattled the ground.

"I can't let you keep making a mess of this town the way you have been. You have been getting away with this for too long," I said, trying to keep my voice steady.

"You will regret getting in the way of Hajime Dai the Basilisk," he said with a laugh.

"The Basilisk?" I questioned.

He stepped back in disbelief that I didn't know who he was. He studded himself and stood back up straight.

"Yes, I am one of the twelve Black Zodiac members. You have never heard of us?" he said with a nervous laugh.

"I have heard of the Black Zodiac, but never thought we would meet till now," I said, keeping my balance and holding on to hilt of my sword.

"Thanks to that stupid leader of the seven swords, he was never able to make the bonds that he needed to create the seven strongest weapons." He laughed. "He killed everyone for revenge, so it helped us crawl from the dark and into the real world." He looked at me and gave another grin.

I tried not to let him know I was Manchu the Dragon. Tried to keep my face serious. I was confused with how he knew more about what I was supposed to do than I did. *How does he have all this information. What does he mean by purified weapons and bonds? How can there only be seven weapons that can do the transformation?* My head was starting to spin with all the questions that grew inside me. I had thirteen members; I mean, I killed most of them, but still seven out of thirteen people. How was that possible?

"You, man with the blue eyes like the water, who are you? I should know the name of the man I will be killing," he spoke.

"My name is Junjie Manchu," I said with confidence.

"Never heard of you," he said and then jumped toward me.

I was expecting him to do that. I unsheathed my sword. A bright light blinded me as I stopped his weapon in midair. I didn't think he was expecting that. He wasn't smiling anymore. The sparks were exploding as both weapons were holding each other back. My blade looked the same, but it looked sharper, like it could cut a single strand of hair if that was what I wanted to do. I felt a strange power enter my body. It felt warm and peaceful. As we held our position, a spark touched my clothing on the sleave of my hanfu.

My clothing started to glow. Before my very eyes, my clothing was changing. Another flash of light. I closed my eyes. The flash made my opponent jump back. I was in shock. When the light faded, I opened my eyes as a gust of wind blew by. My hanfu was now a flame of glittering vibrates. It looked as though it was on fire. I was wearing a crown, a red ruby in the center of my forehead that came up into something that looked like two horns on both sides. My hair turned red.

My sword was no longer see-through. It was covered in flame in my right hand. I pulled my sword closer to my face so I could see it. I thought it would burn, but I was welcomed with warmth. As I looked at the sword, I saw my eyes were no longer calm like the ocean. They were crimson. I had never felt so much power. Was this the power of the petrified weapons? I grabbed my sword with both hands and stood in my pose, ready to fight this giant man who needed to be stopped. I felt so confident. He looked at me and laughed loudly. I could see a dark, pulsating light surround him.

"You are the dragon. You look cute with all your flames and horns, but you have no idea what I have in store for you. This will be the end of the leader of the seven swords. I hope you welcome death," he spoke.

I watched as his body absorbed the dark aura that covered his body. This dark mass covered almost the whole town. The only part it didn't cover was where I was standing. I guess the light from my sword kept the dark energy away from me.

He devoured it in a matter of seconds. His body was starting to get distorted. He started to get bigger and taller. The horns on his mask grew with him. When he was done transforming, he looked like a giant bull that stood on two legs. He had hooves, and his whole body was covered in hair.

His hands still looked like hands, but furry. His weapon looked like a spoon in his hands. A rope appeared around the end of his weapon. With one hand, he wiped the rope around his neck and wore it as a necklace. He stood, looking at me for a moment with his eyes black as night, then lunged at me.

He was quick. I barely had time to dodge his attack. I jumped to the top of one of the buildings next to me. After the dirt cleared, I saw a huge hole in the ground where I once stood. Before I even knew it, he was behind me. He struck me in the back, his claws sharp. I could feel the blood starting to drip down my back.

I lost my footing and fell from the rooftop into the hole. I rolled over to look out of the hole. I saw him getting prepared to do his final attack. Barley being able to move, I braced myself for impact. As he jumped, I saw a bright light then a jerk on my clothing. Then I felt the air on my face as though I was flying. I saw blue hair swaying in the breeze.

Whoever it was gently landed on the ground then dropped me on the ground. I hit my head on the hard, rough ground. The pain shot through my body, then I heard her voice.

"You are always a fool. You never change, do you? For a leader, you know nothing," she hissed.

I got up off the ground and rubbed the back of my head and saw Lee standing there. She was holding a crystal bow in her hand, and it was laying sideways in her hand. A bright light came from her bow. Suddenly it was Sky, her viper. I was stunned to know her weapon was her pet and that she also had a purified weapon. I was also confused to why she had saved me. She hated me back then. I knew she hated me now.

"You can't fight them all alone like you did before. We are all matched up and paired with who we can defeat," she said as she looked at me with her cold eyes.

"What do you mean we are matched up?" I said, confused.

"I mean we can only fight the zodiac that our sign is meant for." She rolled her eyes and continued, "If I wouldn't have stepped in, Junjie, you would have died a fool. I don't know why you can never learn a lesson. You would have thought you would have learned after the first time. These Black Zodiac, what a dumb name," she whispered to herself as she saw me smirking at her comment.

I swore I saw her blush with embarrassment, but that was short-lived. She glared at me and looked away. I felt like this was the first time I had seen Lee.

Her hair was light blue, like the sky on a summer day. It looked like her hair could be mid-of-her-back length. I couldn't tell, as it blew through the wind. Her eyes were blue, with a unique green to them. Her small body looked so fragile, looked like she could be a porcelain doll. Her skin was so light. She was wearing short black shorts with leggings and a gray tank top. *Is everyone different now?* I wondered.

"You are a fool. We must meet up with Light soon. He has more information for you," she said as she walked past me.

I followed behind her. We didn't talk the rest of the way to Light's house. It seemed like the quiet walk took forever. Walking through the woods was very peaceful. I felt like the first time in a long time. The birds singing in the distance distracted my mind from everything else going on.

Whatever Light wanted to talk to me about was always important, and I wasn't sure if I was ready to do all this fighting again; but then again, I wanted to help all the people it was affecting. At that moment, I pictured what I witnessed in the town square.

Just then, I heard Light's voice in the distance. He was waving. I couldn't really hear what he was saying, but he looked older and more defined and handsome. His hair no longer looked like he had cat ears. His long silver hair was pulled back in a ponytail that went to his waist, and he had two long bangs that went to his chin on the left side of his head.

He was wearing a kimono that was black, with waves painted on it. The top of the kimono was open, so you could see the rugged shape of his body. He was way more built than he was before. You could see the gems of sweat that slowly dripped down his chest and to his rock-hard pecks, down to his six-pack that the shirt almost covered. It looked as though he was training, and that's why he had it open.

He didn't have any facial hair, which made him look younger than he was. His eyes were a soft gold color. It looked like his weapon hadn't changed. He still had his silver tiger claws shining in the sun as he waved at us. I saw him put his arms down and start to come toward us. As he did, his weapon just faded till it was no longer there anymore.

"It took you long enough to get here," he said as he laughed. His voice was different and a bit deeper. Before I could answer, Lee did it for me.

"This fool thought he would play with the Basilisk," she said with a sigh.

"How did that go?" he asked.

"Not very well. He would have died if I didn't step in and save him, Light," she told him.

"What is it that you wanted to tell me, Light?" I asked.

"That's just it. Lee tried as well to go against the Fallen Demon, and she couldn't beat him either. There is only one explanation. We need to find the other warriors that follow with us. We have you, Cherry, Lee, Tomi Ty, and myself."

I interrupted him before he could finish. "Are you saying I must find all the zodiac I killed? How is that possible?" I questioned him, almost in shock.

"Yes, I think that our powers go to someone else once we die till it finds someone worthy," he said with pain in his eyes.

"So another person has to stand up to sacrifice themselves..." I couldn't even fathom the thought.

"Yes, I believe it won't end till the world is safe from all the bad and darkness that is in this world, so maybe if we can destroy this dark zodiac that have come out of the ground to start havoc, we can finally end this. It won't be easy to defeat them. I know them, and they only use people and create problems for each other." Light's eye's started to fill with water as he tried to hide it with a smile.

I didn't know what to do. I knew about Light's dark past, and I knew he must think this was all his fault, but it wasn't. I did believe that he had more to tell in his story though. I felt like he wanted to say more but didn't or couldn't. I hoped he wouldn't hide it forever. There might be something more I would have to know.

Maybe later down the road, he would finally tell us the whole story. Light turned his back toward us. I watched as the waves moved in the wind on his kimono. I was about to step forward to place my hand upon his shoulder, and that was when I felt a yank back on my arm. I looked back, and it was Lee. She looked serious. I'd never seen her look so terrifying. Whatever it was, she was serious.

"So, Light, where do we start with this?" I thought I would, as I was still getting a stern look from Lee.

"We must find the others. Cherry and I were together for a while after you got control of your sword, but it didn't work out between us. So she may be back at her home in the fields again." Light sighed heavily.

"So I guess we will make our way to the fields and find her. Even though we don't know if the dark Zodiac got to her yet or Ty yet. So we may even be going for no reason at all. Maybe even find one of our dead allies." Lee said.

"It's a chance we must take to save everyone not just ourselves. We may fall trying are you both prepared to lose your lives this time?" Light questioned us.

There was a moment of silence as we looked at each other. Lee looked sure she was ready for this. The thing that made me hesitate was Light. His voice didn't sound sure. His voice trembled every time he spoke. I could definitely go through with this and die for what I had done to everyone before this and pay for my choices.

119

Could I put Light and Lee through it though? Light turned and looked at me. His eyes looked at me with the most intensity, like he knew what I was thinking, and that look made me know for a fact he was ready to risk everything to save everyone from these horrible people that had been unlashed into this world.

I felt all the doubt fall from my mind. I gave Light a smile and a nod. If I had them, I knew we could do anything. These people needed to go. We were the only ones that could do anything about it, so we will or die trying.

That night, we made our way through the forest. It was a dark night. It reminded me of that night so long ago when I lost my family. The one night that changed my life forever. I watched Light as he walked in front of me. Lee walked closely beside him. They were talking about something I could barely hear.

I wasn't worried about their small talk; I was more concerned of running into another one of the Black Zodiacs than I was of them. It'd been so long since I was out walking with Light, having another adventure, I guess you could put it.

I was remembering how it was, where Cherry lived the green fields that went on for miles, the flowers that bloomed there that smelled like a sweet strawberry and kiwi mixed. All the herbs planted next to the cabin. Where she would go to get the stuff to make her healing mixtures.

Light had always had a thing for her. They were together for a moment. I always wondered what had happened. Cherry and I stopped talking shortly after. It was probably because I became so distant. I was happy to be able to see her again even though it was nerve-racking as well. I didn't really know what to say now that we were being thrown into battle again. On top of that, we had to find all the warriors again and hope they would join us.

There was an opening in the woods, where Light and Lee were standing there still. I was confused since we should have been close to Cherry's cabin. I saw an opening between Light and Lee. I saw flames on the cabin. I was eminently thrown back into my mind when I was young with my family and how I lost them, my father and sister laying on the floor, with arrows through their chests; my mother scooping me up and running out of the house as the cabin was ingulfed in flames.

"What the hell happened here?" Lee said.

Her voice broke me from my horrifying memory. I walked closer to see what she was talking about. The stunning fields had deep rivets. It looked as though someone had taken a giant knife to the ground and made deep cuts into the earth. The flames were mixing with the sky as the sun went down. The orange, red, and yellows danced in the sky together. The cabin had already collapsed.

I was wondering where Cherry was and if she was still alive. We heard a loud noise from behind the dancing flames in the distance. We quickly ran over to see Cherry fighting one of the Black Zodiacs. He was still covered with his cape. He thrusted toward her. As his cape fell, I saw a short-haired man, with brown hair the color of chocolate. His eyes were the color of the sunset. His weapon were these long nails that were fixated to his nails. They looked as though they were made of lava. The way he moved after her was like a dance.

I watched Cherry with her nine tails around to keep her body protected from this beast. I saw a flash of light. Before I knew it, Light was standing in front of Cherry, with his claws out. I saw another flash of light as Light's tiger claws started to change.

It looked as though the waves on Light's cloth engulfed his body when the waves stopped. Light was wearing a kimono that was open in the chest. His bottoms and top were a beautiful, misty blue color. All the metal that were used to hold his tiger claws had disappeared. It looked as though his claws were coming out of his hands. They were now crystal. They were a sky-blue color. His long silver hair had a hint of blue to it. He held his ground against this stranger.

I saw the caped man jump back. He stood there for a moment, looking at Light, and then ran off. I looked back at Light, and he was back to normal. He was hugging Cherry and asking if she was okay. Lee walked toward Light with a smile on her face, like she might or might not know something we didn't know.

That was Lee for you though. I had never felt so far apart from everyone like I had in that moment. Light and Lee seemed to get along way better than I did. Even Cherry and I hadn't really spoken since Saki…

The only thing I wanted to do now was to become closer to everyone. Even Light seemed distant lately. I felt like I had just turned my back on too many of my friends while I was trying to get over what I did. We needed to grow stronger together more than we ever had before. I looked at Light, and he looked back to me with a smile, so warming and welcoming. Like he knew what I was thinking the whole time. I knew Light, and I would always be close with my best friend and my first friend. I wouldn't shut him out anymore. I needed him more than ever.

"Junjie, it is time to go. We must find the others and get Cherry someplace safe. What do you say we go to an inn for the night? The ladies can get their own room, and you and I can get a room. Maybe get a bite to eat, and we can sit down and talk about what is going on together," he said with a kind tone.

"That sounds good!" I felt like I needed a better understanding of what was going on really.

We made our way to the next town over; it was a beautiful little town. It had a waterfall you passed through to enter. There was a river that passed through the town, which gave it a calming, peaceful feeling. You wouldn't know where to find this place unless you had been there before. Light found it quite easily. There were shops on both sides of the river. I was in awe with this mystery of a town I had never known. Cherry hadn't spoken the whole way here. I was wondering what was on her mind.

"There it is the Dragon's Lair Inn."

Light pointed to a large bridge that looked like it was made of ivory. It looked so smooth you could slide right off it if you made the wrong move. It was carved into a dragon; you walked the dragon's body, and the inn was at the top of its head. Golden outlining covered its scales. A light blue colored its body. The horns on its head looked as though they were trees blessing the earth.

We started to make our way across. It was breathtaking. I had never seen anything like it before. Part of me was excited to be in this new area with everyone. It felt as though I could finally be in peace with myself and my mistakes. Lee stepped ahead of me and looked at me as though she wanted to talk. Which was odd. She never really cared to talk to me since I first met her.

"Hey, Junjie, Cherry and I are heading up to the inn. I will book the rooms and have everything ready before you two get up there," Light said with a light grin.

"Okay, Light, I will see you up there," I replied.

Lee and I watched them walk away. She waited till they were a good distance away. This bridge looked as though it was two to three miles long. She looked at me again and started to walk. I started following behind her.

"Junjie, you need to pull yourself together," she hissed.

"What do you mean?" I replied, trying to sound clueless.

"You know exactly what I mean, Junjie. You can't keep looking in the past for answers. There are no answers there, only questions. You can't become who you want in the past. Your soul has been purified from the darkness that once held you captive. We all know the you that did that to Saki wasn't you. Light tried to see a different path for you, but that is something we all had to go through to get to this point and become stronger," she said in a soft, calming voice.

"You mean Light knew I would kill her and didn't stop me?" I yelled.

"He tried to help you. Nothing is as it seems, Junjie. A time will come when you will know everything. Light was too busy trying to fight the other zodiac warriors to get to you in time. The reason I didn't join you at that point is because Light asked me not to at that time. Maybe he saw my death on the horizon. Don't let your yesterday bleed into your today. You're walking around blind right now. We all are. Light has to carry the burden of knowing what could have happened and what can happen. We all must be strong from this point on," she spoke.

"I know he has a lot to bear, but it also makes me wonder what he is hiding or how much we know. He is my best friend, so I know, having his power, he must also keep some things quiet and to himself. I just wish I could know more or what side he is really on." I swallowed hard, knowing what I just said. "But really, most of his past is a secret. He has told me some of it, yes, but I'd like to know more. I'd like to hold some of his burden on my shoulders." My eyes started to tear up. "I know I don't deserve it. I was gone for so long and kept everyone locked out for so long that I barley know any of you anymore. You I never really knew you other than you hated me." I finished speaking.

"You may never know me, but I know you and have seen how much you have grown and what you went through to get that sword and get to where you are now," she said as I looked at her, shocked.

I was about to say something, but before I could, she placed her finger over my mouth, and her Sky was looking at me. Her viper sky had wrapped herself around Lee's hand like she normally did, but I felt like Sky was giving me a warning. Lee's beautiful teal eyes shined as she looked at me harshly.

"You will know my story when I think it's time you can handle it. Right know isn't the time, Junije," she said as we continued to walk.

We walked in silence for the rest of the way. Halfway through the walk, the sun started to set. It was an amazing sight, seeing the treetops and the towns in the distance. I felt like an ant in a much bigger world. If I had wings, I would have felt like I could fly right off. In the distance, I saw a town that looked like it was getting started for a festival in quite a big area. I was hoping that maybe we could all go there for a little fun. I knew it was foolish to think when we had so much work to do. I didn't realize how much the world grew as I sat in my sorrows. Before I knew it, we were at the end of the bridge.

The whole cliff top was filled with lights that looked stars. The inn sat in the darkest corner of the cliff top. It made sense to keep it hidden at night just in case the barrier didn't cover that area. The inn was very nice. It was made out of ivory as well and had the same colors as the bridge. It also appeared to look like a dragon.

Around the doorway, the two long beams were made of ivory scales with the gold outline. When I got to the door, the door looked like it was made of gold and was pretty heavy. It was defiantly heavier than it looked. When you opened the door, there was the office on the left-hand side. It was made of wood; it looked like red wood.

Following the wall to the right, there was a spiral staircase that led up to the rooms. Behind the stairs was a restaurant called the Red Dragon. There were several round glass tables with gold legs. I saw Light and Cherry sitting at a table in the corner. Lee must have seen them before I did because she started walking toward the table and sat down.

I followed behind her. I noticed the steps on the staircase were made of some kind of crystal. It looked as though it had molting lava glowing in the stone. I also saw some red flowers I'd never seen before. It looked like they were made of fire. They moved so calmly. It seemed to compliment the red rose and the gold trim of the walls. When I sat down at the table, Light handed me a menu and smiled.

ABOUT THE AUTHOR

Arminda Eisenhardt is a single mother of four who lives in Ohio. She is hardworking and loves to write short stories in her free time. It is her true passion.

Printed in the USA
CPSIA information can be obtained
at www.ICGtesting.com
CBHW030252081024
15373CB00046BB/963